MAZES OF THE MIND

MIKE SHERER

To Wendy Vogel,
for all of the priceless writing wisdom and skills
she freely shared with the writing group she led
for years — Cincinnati Fiction Writers

1

A MOONLESS NIGHT *showcasing a multitude of stars. The air is still, the earth is still. Dark mountains loom in all directions. The shadowless void is quiet. No roads, no paths, only a dry gulley leading up. The sandy irregular ground is forbidding treacherous terrain. This could be any century, any millennium. The desert landscape is eternal on human scale. Nothing alive stirs here.*

Except one thing. A dark form rises up from the ground like a resurrection. Yet it is not a clumsy movie zombie; it moves slowly, cautiously, so as not to disturb the cat's whiskers of the night. The dark being creeps forward, hunched, its tread as noiseless as that of a hologram. This could be the shadow of a cloud skittering across the sand. It pauses, listens, looks about, senses all around, then advances again, repeating this at a patternless pace as it moves up a dry gulley.

This misshapen creature resembles a giant bug. It is hunchbacked. There is a strange carapace on its head. It carries a long object like a segmented insect leg. Despite all these irregularities, its movements are so smooth it could be fashioned of silicone.

Noiseless movement shuffles forward behind it. There are a dozen more like this erratically advancing creature scuttling across the ground, just as muffled, just as misshapen. This odd pack makes its patient way up the gulley.

The dark shape leading this eerie entourage comes to a large rock. It crouches and raises a hand. The others flatten, disappearing into the ground. The one in front extends its shell-topped head around the rock to peer ahead into a void. He removes the hump from his back — a backpack — and extracts a small device. A cyclopean metallic eye glows greenly with night vision capability. It is focused on a void within the void, a blacker shade of black, an ebony ovoid. The entrance to a cave.

A brilliant flash of blinding light. A man's face fills the cave entrance.

●   ●   ●

The light dims, leaving only the face. It is battered, scarred, irregular gashes crusted with blood, bruises fading to all colors of the rainbow. Both eyes are blackened. Both lips split and swollen. Nose broken, straightened, broken again. Gaps where teeth once were. Hair Waring-blendered. A week's growth of whiskers probably conceals many more injuries.

The image of the cave entrance resolves into a mirror. The beaten face is inches from the glass. The man is leaning into the mirror, eyes scrutinizing each injury, darting from wound to wound. He shifts his weight, leans back. He had been leaning on a wooden dresser upon balled fists, balanced on his knuckles. He straightens. Now more of him can be seen in the mirror. His reflected bare chest and shoulders and arms are as bruised and scarred as his face.

He steps further back, still staring into the mirror. He is clad only in gray undershorts, which means many more injuries are to be seen. Studying them in the mirror, he turns this way and that. He concentrates on his reflected image, as if afraid to see the unfiltered actual damage that has been done to his body.

At last, he turns away from the mirror. The small dresser holding the mirror is ornately-carved dark wood, perhaps mahogany. A matching wardrobe stands in a corner of this small room. A shelf on the wall holds books and bottles of liquor. There is a small double bed. A rickety nightstand with a rickety dim lamp. The low ceiling would oppress a tall man. Light seeps into the tight dim room around the edges of closed floor-to-ceiling wooden shutters.

As the man crosses to them, he glances down to find he is treading on a worn wooden floor. He unlatches the shutters and slides them open. Brilliant light impales his wide-open pupils.

•   •   •

Brilliant light issues from a spotlight just above his face. He squeezes his eyes closed and turns his head away. Yet the light is so strong it pierces the thin membrane of his eyelids, illuminating the mad pattern of red blood vessels within them. And the light seems to penetrate no matter how he averts his face.

•   •   •

The man turns away from the unshuttered floor to ceiling glass patio door. The incendiary daylight outside this dark cave of a room is too much, it burns all the exposed trauma on his bare skin. Looking away, he can open his eyes enough to blink them, again and again, letting his pupils adjust in brief flashes. Finally, the haziness thins, the room comes back into focus. The dark shadows have been dispelled; the cramped confines grow more solid. The bed is in disarray. Clothes are piled on a wooden straight-back chair. On the nightstand a pack of cigarettes and book of matches beside a dirty ashtray.

The man walks to the wardrobe and opens it. Inside he finds men's clothes hanging — some sporting, some casual day wear, some formal evening wear. Several pairs of men's shoes are below — tennis shoes, loafers, dress shoes.

He crosses back to the dresser. Avoiding the mirror, he opens a drawer and finds men's underwear and socks. Opening another drawer, he finds something more interesting. A passport. He snatches it up. It was issued by Great Britain. Inside, a photo of his face, what he looks like without all the damage. Also, a name. Saxon Hedges. An address in London. He flips through the many stamps. European Union, Nigeria, Japan, Russia, United States, Afghanistan, Indonesia, Algeria, Canada, Philippines, Pakistan.

The man has a name now. Saxon Hedges. Saxon replaces the passport and picks up a wallet. It is stuffed with Euros and pounds and dollars. Also, a British ID card with his photo and a London address. And a snapshot of a football team.

•　　　•　　　•

Saxon, wearing a uniform like the ones in the photo, kicks a ball around with other men dressed in the same uniform.

•　　　•　　　•

Saxon stares at the photo. His teammates? None of the faces look familiar. In a surge of panic, he casts a frantic glance around the room. Nothing looks familiar. With a force of will, he concentrates on the photo once again. On his own image. This face is not beaten up. He wasn't injured like this playing football. This was taken before whatever happened to him happened. Had he been mugged? In a car wreck? Fallen from a six-story building?

Saxon slips the photo back into the wallet, replaces the wallet in the drawer next to the passport, closes the drawer. He walks into a compact bathroom. Cuts on the bright light, leans on the sink and peers into the mirror on the wall. This face has been massacred. With shaking hands he snatches up a glass on the sink and storms out to the wall shelf. Opens a bottle of whiskey and pours the glass full. Chugs.

•   •   •

Saxon, in his soccer uniform, is in a crowded English pub with his teammates. They are all dirty, bruised and muddy. It is loud and raucous, with everyone knocking together pints of ale and chugging, apparently celebrating a win.

•   •   •

Saxon sets the empty glass down. He can breathe cleanly, and his eyes aren't watering. So he is used to drinking hard liquor. He turns back to the open shutters with a squint. His eyes have adjusted enough for him to endure the bright outdoors.

Saxon opens the door and steps outside onto a small balcony. He hugs himself as a brisk wind comes down out of the mountains. Looking down from the distant peaks, he sees he is on the second floor of an old two-story building of east European style. Below is a small courtyard café on a narrow cobblestone lane. Several people in light jackets and sweaters sit drinking coffee. At the front of the small collection of tables a violin player is performing. Saxon closes his eyes.

•   •   •

The same strains of violin music echo through the dark. Echoes? From a small confined space? A cave?

•   •   •

Saxon opens his eyes. He has heard this music before. Dvorak's Ninth. The New World Symphony, or at least the violin part. Had he heard a recording of it? This now is one man playing one violin, outside, with no echoes. But it is the same music, he is sure of it. The violinist glances up at him over the top of his violin held to just below his chin, smiles briefly, then looks back to his scant audience.

Which includes a man seated at a table manipulating a wooden puppet. It jerks all across the tabletop.

•   •   •

Saxon, in blood-soaked military fatigues, is drug by the arms through the night by two dark figures. His bruised and bloody body jerks like the puppet. He screams in agony as his wounded limp broken body is drug without care across rocky ground.

•   •   •

"Good morning, Saxon."

Saxon whirls around at the French accent behind him. Just inside the room stands a short slight wisp of a man clad in shirt and slacks, pale-complexioned, with collar-length jet black hair. He stares at Saxon with a blank expression as he raises a cigarette to his lips, draws deeply on it.

•   •   •

Saxon lies naked, face up, tied to a bed. His body is covered with scars just like the ones on his face. His battered face is twisted in fear and agony as he stares up. The glowing end of a cigarette descends by increments of eternity from out of the dark. After the passing of an age it touches his bare chest. Saxon screams!

•   •   •

Startled by the intensity of the memory, Saxon lunges back against the railing. He starts to pitch over it. The newcomer dashes out onto the balcony to catch Saxon. But all Saxon can see is the glowing cigarette coming at him, toward his bare chest, like in the memory. Saxon grabs the rail with his right hand, catching himself, then slashes out with his left to grab the man's wrist. "Keep that away from me!" Saxon twists the wrist, forcing the man to drop his cigarette.

The man winces. "All right, Saxon. You win. Like always. I'm no athlete. No footballer. Like you."

•   •   •

Saxon, in his team shorts and jersey, charges down a playing field dribbling a ball. He is running flat out as he maneuvers the ball with his feet with impressive skill.

•　　　•　　　•

Saxon freezes, remembering. The man makes no move to escape. He studies the damaged convolutions of Saxon's face while waiting. At last, the face relaxes and Saxon releases the wrist. He stares at the man, trying to puzzle out who he is. When the man steps back, rubbing his sore wrist, Saxon's inquisitive voice probes. "Philip?"

Philip smiles. "Big improvement over yesterday." He crushes the still-lit cigarette with his shoe.

"I'm an athlete? A football player?"

•　　　•　　　•

A player from the opposing team charges at Saxon as he dribbles the ball down the side of the field.

•　　　•　　　•

"You are getting better." Philip nods toward the room. "This calls for a drink." He walks back inside.

Saxon starts to follow, but glances down at the crushed cigarette. He kicks it off the balcony with his bare foot then follows Philip into the room. He closes the door and shutters behind him, returning the room to comforting dimness. As he turns back around, Philip fires a shot glass at him from the wall shelf. Saxon catches it.

"Reflexes seem okay." Philip pours himself a shot from the whiskey bottle. "Sorry, there's no ale, or beer of any kind."

Saxon steps up beside him, fingering the shot glass. "I'll have what you're having." He hands the glass back to Philip.

Philip pours another shot. "If nothing else, your taste has improved." Philip offers the glass, and Saxon takes it with his other hand. "I didn't know you were ambidextrous."

Saxon looks at the hand holding the glass. "I didn't know that, either."

"Still, you seem to be doing better than yesterday."

Saxon studies Philip's composed face. "I'm not doing as good as you seem to think I am. Start from square one."

Philip smiles. "Square two. We were at square one yesterday. Today you know my name and that you play football." He turns away to inspect the books on the shelf with the liquor bottles. "Last game of the season. Bozidar hit you so hard …"

•   •   •

Saxon, in his team shorts and jersey, charges down the field dribbling a ball. A player from the other team charges toward him. Saxon passes the ball off at the last second. But neither he nor the charging player can change course. He and Saxon collide! Head to head! Crack!

•   •   •

"… you were out for ten minutes."

•   •   •

Saxon is on the ground flat on his back staring up at the gathered concerned faces of his teammates staring down at him.

•   •   •

"You walked off the field …"

•   •   •

Saxon limps off the field, supported by a teammate on either side. Philip paces the sidelines, looking anxiously at Saxon as he nears.

•   •   •

"… but you were out on your feet. Your fourth concussion. Sax, it's time for you to retire from the game."

Saxon sits on the edge of the bed, suddenly weary, as if the effort of remembering has exhausted him. "Yeah. I remember. Some of it."

Philip picks up one slim volume from the shelf and turns toward the bed. "What's the last thing you remember?"

Saxon frowns. "I was dreaming. I was walking. In the mountains." He glances up at the closed shutters. "Not these mountains. It was in the desert. At night."

"Yes?"

"That's it. My head's so fuzzy." Saxon chugs his drink in a single gulp, like before. Like before, this doesn't faze him.

"You cracked heads with Bozidar. Apparently, his is much harder than yours." Philip sets his glass down. "Don't worry. It will come back to you. In the meantime, relax. Take in Prague." Philip tosses the book he holds. "Read a good book."

Saxon catches it. "So you are babysitting me. In Prague. Why?"

Philip sighs. "I told you why yesterday and I'll probably tell you again tomorrow. I hope I'm not telling you a week from now. This could become very tiresome."

"Why!?"

"The match was in Prague. I volunteered to stay behind with you until you were able to travel." He sighs more heavily than before. "We've been friends all our lives, Sax."

•　　•　　•

Saxon, in his soccer uniform, is celebrating in the crowded English pub with his teammates. He raises a mug of ale to the person seated beside him. Which is Philip, in street clothes. Saxon chugs his ale, while Philip drinks a glass of whiskey.

•　　•　　•

Recognition registers amid the scars on Saxon's face.

Philip smiles in response. "Just relax, Sax. This is going to take some time. But I'm here for the duration, however long it takes." Philip finishes his drink. "I'm going down to the café. Get dressed and join me." He walks out, closing the door behind him.

Saxon stares at the closed door for a moment then glances down at the book he holds. It is printed in the original Czech. Surprised that he can read it, he mouths the words on the cover. "'The Metamorphosis', by Franz Kafka." He opens the cover. Inside is a smashed bug. Not an illustration of one, but an actual flattened bug. A cockroach.

• • •

A cockroach scurries across the floor. A hand snatches it up out of sight. A second later there is a loud SLAP.

• • •

Saxon, disturbed, stares at the squashed bug. Finally, he flips through several pages to the beginning. He reads aloud the first sentence. "As Gregor Samsa awoke one morning from uneasy dreams he found himself transformed in his bed into a gigantic insect." Disturbed even more, he slaps the book closed. Realizing it has made the same sound as the one in his memory, he opens the book and slaps it closed again and again.

Saxon slaps the book closed one last time and sets it down on the nightstand. He stands and walks up to the dresser to stare at his reflection in the mirror. The image in the mirror changes, transforms to his game face, sweaty and grimy and reddened from exertion. It changes again, with streaks of camouflage grease and topped by a military helmet. It changes again, to the bruised and battered face he had awakened to. He smiles. "It sure must have been a long hard season." He goes to the wardrobe to select some clothes.

2

A FEW MINUTES LATER, Saxon emerges from the small inn onto the cobblestone courtyard. It is a chilly spring day, a good excuse for him wearing long sleeves and long pants that conceal his injuries. As he approaches the dozen tables set up before the café he searches for Philip. He is nowhere to be seen. The puppeteer Saxon had spied from his balcony is still at the same table. He makes his puppet dance across the tabletop. Saxon watches for a moment. The puppet seems hand-carved, and well made. The hands of the elderly man manipulating it are more dexterous than you would assume from their gnarled appearance. He smiles up at Saxon. "It's for sale."

It takes a moment for Saxon to realize the old man has spoken to him in Czech. And that he has understood him.

The puppeteer continues in Czech. "I have many more. At my shop." He nods off down the street. "Two blocks."

Saxon stammers, in Czech. "It's beautiful."

The old man's smile disappears. "It wasn't meant to be beautiful." The puppeteer jerks the strings, making his puppet lurch in violent spasms across the table toward Saxon.

•   •   •

Saxon, strapped face-up in only undershorts on a table, jerks spasmodically like the puppet is doing. He is reacting to being shocked with an electric prod held by shadowy hands. The prod is withdrawn, and the spasms subside. But the music doesn't subside, the horrid screeching of the detested violin. Saxon is shocked again, and again, his screams matching the screams of the violin strings as body flesh flings itself against the heavy leather straps restraining it.

•   •   •

Saxon jerks back from the advancing puppet. Into the table behind, upsetting a chess board. The two elderly men playing grab the board, the pieces, trying to preserve their game.

Saxon apologizes, in Czech. "I'm sorry."

The two glare up at him, cursing fluently in Czech.

Saxon turns back to the puppeteer to find him engrossed in making adjustments to his puppet.

"Is there a problem?"

Saxon spins to find a stout middle-age brawler of a man scowling at him. Assuming he is a waiter, Saxon replies in the Czech he was addressed in. "No. Yes. I'm looking for my friend. A young Frenchman. Phillip?"

The waiter continues to glare. "No Frenchman. No Phillip. What do you want here?"

"A cup of coffee?"

Getting no further reaction from the waiter, Saxon lumbers about the tables, searching for Phillip. The waiter, the two chess players, and the puppeteer all watch him. The violin player begins a new tune. Saxon realizes it is Dvorak's Humoresque Number Seven.

●   ●   ●

This same tune blasts as Saxon, in only undershorts, his exposed skin scored with cuts and contusions and burns, is huddled in brilliant light in a heap within a small steel cage.

●   ●   ●

Saxon drifts toward the violinist even as the lilting yet mournful tune unsettles him even more. Yet he cannot not listen.

When the violin player concludes the short piece and sets his instrument aside, Saxon quivers with relief, and resumes scanning the courtyard for Phillip. His darting eyes settle on a young woman seated alone at a table. She is tall and lanky, dressed in a form-fitting dress the same shade as her coal-black hair, a black hat partially concealing her face as she sips black coffee and smokes while engrossed with her phone.

●   ●   ●

Saxon and a black-haired female of the same dimensions are naked in bed engaged in exuberant sex, with her on top. He jerks and thrashes beneath her, same as he had while being shocked. With a laugh, she tosses her hair back, revealing her face. It is the woman seated before him.

●   ●   ●

Saxon staggers back under the force of the vivid memory. He overturns a chair, crashes against a table. The woman looks up at the disturbance. She stares with disdain at Saxon, while he stares back in slack-jawed wonder. She dismisses him with a flick of her cigarette, then looks back down to her phone. Saxon focuses on the cigarette in her hand.

●   ●   ●

The long feminine fingers holding a cigarette have long bright red nails. The glowing end of the cigarette touches Saxon's bare chest. He screams.

•   •   •

Saxon stares at the cigarette the long feminine fingers with bright red nails are holding. She continues to ignore him, busy with her phone. Saxon's legs give way, and he sits heavily into a chair.

"I suggest you leave." The waiter towers above him.

"I'm not drunk. I'm … I'm not well." The waiter continues to glare without sympathy. Saxon's shaky legs raise him upright. The woman takes no notice of him as she is still engrossed with her phone. Saxon staggers away from the tables.

He sees Phillip stride briskly into the inn. "Phillip!" The Frenchman disappears inside without acknowledging him. Saxon rushes in after. No sign of Phillip. Saxon hurries into the lobby. No one other than the desk clerk is present. Saxon hastens to the front desk. "A Frenchman just came in," he inquires in English. "Did you see him?"

The desk clerk stares blankly as he responds in heavily-accented English. "No. No one."

"I just saw him!" The desk clerk shrugs. Saxon turns away, dashing here and there, searching. He ducks into a small gift shop. The female store clerk looks up at him from behind the counter with a smile. He attempts to return the smile, fails. Finding no one else present, he ducks back out.

Saxon walks to the closed doors of the restaurant and tries the knob. The doors are locked. He peers inside. Waiters are setting elegant tables, while a young woman practices on a harp set up in the front of the room. A nearby waiter looks up at the sound of him rattling the door. He bolts away.

Saxon hurries down into a small cellar nightclub. The doors are open, but the room is dark and empty. He looks about, then ducks back out and up the stairs.

Saxon walks back up to the lobby to a female tour operator seated at a small desk in a corner. The desk is covered with pictures and info sheets of available tours. Prominently displayed are pictures of castles, cathedrals, the Astronomical Clock, a small picturesque Medieval village with the name Kutna Hora, the Old Jewish Cemetery. This last snags Saxon's attention. There are many crooked headstones jammed together on top of each other in a small cramped graveyard plot.

•   •   •

Dead naked male bodies are piled atop one another, jammed together like the crooked gravestones displayed on the tour flyer, their faces locked in rictal agony and covered in dried blood that had streamed from their mouths, ears, eyes, noses. Elsewhere, dried blood all around their groins and their buttocks, from where it had flowed copiously out of those orifices. This horror fills Saxon's ever-open eyes while violin music howls in his ever-open ears.

•   •   •

The woman looks up in expectation, speaking in heavily-accented English. "Would you like to book a tour?" Saxon lurches forward and grips the desk with both hands, white-knuckled. He is desperate to hang on. The young woman steps back, fear flickering across her face.

Saxon speaks English, with intense deliberation. "I am looking for someone. A young Frenchman. Have you seen him?"

She shakes her head no.

Saxon sags. "I'm sorry. I'm not well." He stumbles away toward the stairs. The tour operator watches him go from behind her desk. The desk clerk also tracks his progress across the small lobby. Saxon, oblivious to everything other than his exhaustion, slogs up the steps.

Saxon walks the upstairs hallway to a room door. He fishes out an old-fashioned metal room key and inserts it. Nothing. He checks the number on the door. Six. He tries the key again. It won't turn. He jiggles the key in the lock. Nothing. He pulls the key out and pounds on the door. "Phillip! Are you in there!?" He pauses to listen. No sounds from inside the room. He turns away back toward the stairs.

As Saxon limps up to the front desk with his room key in hand, he glances at the tour desk across the lobby. The woman is gone. The desk clerk frowns at his approach. "My room key quit working."

"Are you sure you have the right room?"

"Positive."

"Let me see your key." After Saxon gives him the key, he opens a large ledger. "Mister Saxon Hedges?"

Saxon nods.

"Room twelve?"

"No. Six."

"I have you in room twelve."

Saxon explodes. "I know what room I'm in!"

The desk clerk peers with infinite forbearance into his face. "You're confused. Away from home. In a strange country."

Saxon rubs his forehead, and leans on the front desk. "What about Phillip?"

"The Frenchman?" the desk clerk prompts.

"Yes. Can you check your ledger? Tell me what room he is staying in?"

The desk clerk goes through his ledger. "What is his last name?"

Saxon is stumped. "I … I don't know." He recovers enough to bang the desk with his fist. "There *is* a Phillip staying here!"

The desk clerk's demeanor softens. "A strange place. A foreign country. Too much vodka."

Saxon's voice trembles. "I'm not drunk. And I don't like vodka."

"Then what are you doing with it?"

Saxon stares, at a total loss.

"You've ordered three bottles since you've been here."

Saxon's sigh is nearly a moan.

The desk clerk offers the key back. "I have you booked into room twelve. You have a key to room twelve. Please try it."

Saxon takes the key and stumbles away toward the stairs. By the time he reaches the top step he looks like he is unable to mount another. He glances at room six as he passes. At the door marked twelve he inserts the key. It turns on the first attempt. He opens the door and peers inside. The room looks identical to the one he was in before. He enters and closes the door behind him.

Saxon goes to the dresser and opens the top drawer. His passport is there. He picks it up and flips through it. It is his, without a doubt. He drops it, and the room key and his wallet, into the drawer and closes it. He walks over to the wardrobe and opens it. Same clothes, same shoes. He walks to the wall shelf. Alongside the bottle of whiskey is a nearly-empty bottle of vodka. He walks over to the closed wooden shutters and opens them. The same view as before.

Saxon opens the door and steps out onto the balcony. He gazes down on the courtyard. The woman in black is absent from her table, as is the puppeteer with his puppet. But the two old men are still engaged in their game of chess, and the violinist is playing once again. Bartok's Violin Concerto No. 2.

•　　•　　•

While this same tune blares, Saxon, battered and bruised, sits naked in a small steel cage, collapsed back against the bars with a blank expression. He appears comatose.

•　　•　　•

Saxon turns to go back inside, but something on the floor catches his eye. A partially-smoked stepped-on cigarette.

•　　•　　•

Saxon, in only his undershorts, stares down at the crushed cigarette on the balcony floor he had just forced from Philip's hand,

and that Philip had just stepped on. Saxon kicks it off the balcony with his bare foot.

•   •   •

Saxon squats to inspect the cigarette. He picks it up, looks it over, sniffs it. After studying it long and hard, he walks back into the room with it. He closes the glass door, closes the shutters. He collapses in the blessed dim light and silence onto the bed. He rolls over to carefully place the cigarette in an ashtray on the nightstand. Where he spies the book, "Metamorphosis", by Franz Kafka. He picks the book up and opens it to contemplate the smashed bug. Then he lowers it to contemplate the cigarette butt in the ashtray.

3

A DARK HUMAN FORM *carrying a rifle, with a backpack on his back and a helmet on his head, leading a dozen others like it, moves carefully in a low crouch across barren open ground up a dry gulley toward the entrance to a dark cave. The quiet night erupts in automatic weapon fire! They have been ambushed, caught out in the open by a superior force in the rocks above. A vicious brief firefight. In a few minutes all of the men lie bleeding on the ground. Including the one leading in front. He throws down his gun and raises his hands.*

Dozens of poorly-clad but heavily-armed fighters come down from the rocks, surrounding the dead and wounded men on the ground. They quickly determine which are dead. They roll one wounded man over onto his back. It is Saxon.

The ambushers jerk him and the half-dozen still living to their feet. The ones who can't walk are dragged. Saxon, in ragged fatigues, is drug by two dark figures by the arms across rocky ground. He is in agony, screaming from the pain of his wounds, as his limp bloody body is ripped across the hard ground. They pull him up the dry gulley toward the dark void of a cave entrance.

•   •   •

Saxon sleeps soundly on the bed in the dark quiet room, still dressed as before. Until the door opens and light floods in from the hall. A dark form in the doorway switches on the room light. The intruder is revealed to be a short compact middle-aged black man in a business suit. He strides in. "Saxon! Wake up! You are sleeping your life away."

Saxon opens his swollen eyes, squints at the man looming above him at the side of the bed. "Phillip?"

The stranger laughs. "Do I look like a Philip?" He cuffs Saxon playfully on the ear. "Now get up. I'm starving."

Saxon reacts to the soft blow by springing up out of bed and dropping into a fighting crouch.

The man jumps back, smiling, and drops into a defensive posture. "You don't want to mess with me, Saxon."

Saxon relaxes out of his crouch and rubs his head. "You're right. I don't. I'm sorry." He looks around in a sleep-addled daze. "I knew this wasn't my room."

"Of course it's your room. Sax!"

Irritation wins out over befuddlement. "Quit talking like you know me!"

The intruder stops laughing, grows serious. "Settle down, Saxon. Of course I know you. We've worked together for years."

Saxon studies the man standing before him. "You don't look like a football player."

"No, but you do. That's why you got the work and I didn't."

20

"What work?"

"The World Cup Wonders." He pauses for a light to come on in Saxon's face. It doesn't, so he presses on. "The comedy we're filming in Prague."

• • •

Saxon is on a playing field engaged in a football game, the same memory as before. Only now a film crew can be seen set up on the sideline.

• • •

Saxon's jaw drops. "Are you saying we're actors?"
The laugh returns. "I wish. We're stuntmen."

• • •

Saxon is on the sideline practicing a football move with the stunt coordinator and a real football player.

• • •

Saxon collapses back onto the bed.
"Sax! Get up. I'm starved."
Saxon looks up to the man cajoling him to go eat. "Ben?"

• • •

Saxon stands on the sideline in his football uniform conversing with the man he just called Ben, dressed in the same suit he presently wears.

• • •

The man smiles brighter than before. "At least you remember *something*. But you apparently don't remember how much I dislike you calling me that. My name is Obinna."
"What happened?"

"Dumbest thing I ever heard of. They had you in there doing stunts with real football players. I mean, you may *look* like a football player, but you can't go head to head against real World Cup athletes."

•   •   •

Saxon, in his uniform, charges down the field dribbling a ball. He is running flat out as he maneuvers the ball with his feet, same as before. Only now the film crew can be seen filming the action from the sideline.

•   •   •

"And I do mean head to head. Remember Bozidar?"

•   •   •

Directly in front of the cameras, a player from the opposing team charges toward Saxon. Saxon passes the ball off at the last moment.

•   •   •

"They told him to make it look real. But Boz is no actor. He went at you like he would in a real game."

•   •   •

Neither Saxon nor the hard charging Bozidar can change course in time. He and Saxon collide! Head to head! Crack!!

•   •   •

"Sax, Boz was so sorry for hitting you like that."

•   •   •

The cameras have stopped filming. All activity on the set has stopped as Saxon limps off the field supported by a film crew member on either side. While Obinna paces anxiously along with them, watching Saxon with concern.

•   •   •

"The doctor said you had a concussion. A bad one. And it's not your first. So the film crew left you behind to recover, and I volunteered to stay and look after you." Obinna sits on the bed beside Saxon, with a worried expression. "Can you remember any of it?"

"Bits and pieces."

"So what's the last thing you remember?"

Saxon jerks away. "Phillip asked me that same question."

Obinna laughs. "Yeah, I'm sure a lot of people have been asking you that after the lick you took from Bozidar." He stands. "Get up and clean your face so we can go eat."

"Did my face get beat up like this from working on the football movie?"

"Damn, Sax. One step forward and two steps back." While Saxon merely stares at him, Obinna slaps him on the cheek. When Saxon springs to his feet into a fighting crouch once again, Obinna merely laughs. "Did that hurt?"

Saxon pauses to consider, feeling his cheek where he had just been slapped.

"Your face looks like it's been stomped on. That should have hurt."

Saxon gazes at Obinna, totally lost.

"It's just makeup, buddy. We were trying out a face for your next movie." Obinna barks another laugh. "Did you think it was real? Wouldn't you be hurting like hell if it was?"

Saxon lunges over to the dresser and stares into the mirror. He wipes his right hand roughly across his face. The scars smear, and he doesn't wince with pain.

•   •   •

Saxon's face is smeared with blood.

•   •   •

Saxon turns away to face Obinna. "I've been having flashbacks. To a firefight in the desert."

•   •   •

Saxon, pinned down in the open in the desert at night, blazes away with his automatic rifle, until his body is riddled with bullets.

•   •   •

"*The Caves of Kandahar*. The last movie you worked on before this. There was a battle scene the A-Lister didn't want to dirty his hands with."

Saxon turns back to the mirror. Now all he sees is his face smeared with makeup.

"Can we go eat now? I am so hungry."

Saxon remains at the dresser still staring at his reflection. "Have you seen Phillip?"

"Phillip who?"

Saxon starts toward the door. "I guess he was one of the actors. Or a real football player like Bozidar. I dreamed he was here with me."

"Whoa, Sax." Obinna blocks the door. "You can't go out like that. That face. And they require dress clothes for dinner."

Saxon nods and starts undressing. He uncovers a few fading bruises on his chest and shoulders. He looks up at Obinna.

Who shrugs. "Those look real. It's a rough business we're in."

Tossing his shirt onto the bed, the ashtray catches his eye. He lunges over to look closely at it. The cigarette is gone. He looks back to Obinna still standing before the door. "What happened to the cigarette?"

"When did you start smoking?"

"I don't! But Phillip does. I put a cigarette of his there! Today! Before I went to sleep! Now where is it!?"

Obinna laughs. "Saxon, the clientele here is pretty high-class. I don't think anybody would be sneaking into your room while you're asleep to steal your half-smoked cigarettes, even if they are American."

"Who said anything about it being half-smoked?"

Obinna stops laughing. "Saxon, this is getting wearisome. Get dressed and let's go eat."

Saxon bolts to the door, brushing past him. Yanks it open to stare at the number. Twelve.

"What now?"

Saxon lunges over to the dresser and rummages through the top drawer. He locates a pen and pad of paper. "I'm writing down the room number."

Obinna's good humor returns. "Don't bother." He takes out his phone and snaps a picture of the exterior of the door, then displays it to Saxon. "How's that?"

"I want my own record." He scribbles '12' onto a sheet, then tears it off and goes to stuff it into his pants pocket. Only to realize he has already taken his pants off. He looks to where he had tossed them onto the bed with his shirt.

Obinna's laughter booms. "Shape you're in, this stay could be very entertaining."

Saxon scowls at Obinna as he sticks the slip of paper in his mouth while he pulls a shirt off the hanger and puts it on.

A middle-age couple pass in the hall, glancing in through the open door. The woman smiles at the sight of Saxon with his pants off buttoning his shirt, while the man shakes his head, scowling. Obinna laughs with delight.

4

APPROPRIATELY DRESSED and with a clean face, with Obinna at his side, Saxon strolls into the restaurant he had looked into earlier. The doors are now open and people are dining. At the front of the room is the woman who had been rehearsing on the harp earlier. Saxon scowls at the music, at the musician, as he follows Obinna up to the maitre d'. While Obinna takes care of the seating arrangements, Saxon gazes around. The diners appear well-dressed and well-fed. The waiters appear nimble and efficient. The table settings are elegant, the small cozy room tastefully adorned.

Saxon's perusal is arrested by sighting the black-haired beauty he'd seen earlier at the courtyard cafe. She is wearing an elegant evening gown that emphasizes her long lean form. She sits alone at a table near the middle of the room, smoking a cigarette while paying close attention to the harp player.

•   •   •

Saxon and the woman lie in bed side by side between the sheets, she lazily smoking a cigarette. Saxon studies her, focusing on her long red nails, on the glowing tip of her cigarette.

•   •   •

"We've got a table."

Saxon is startled out of his reverie by Obinna. He starts away following a waiter, but Saxon hangs back, his attention riveted on the woman. "I'll join you in a minute."

Obinna stops to call back over his shoulder. "At least come order."

"I'll have whatever you're having, just half as much."

Obinna sighs in exasperation. Until he follows Saxon's line of sight to the black-haired woman seated alone. He smiles. "Are you sure you're up to it?"

"I'd like to find out."

Obinna nods encouragement then follows the waiter to their table.

After seeing where his companion is seated, Saxon strides up to the woman's table. He stops just behind her.

She speaks without looking, English with a thick Russian accent. "Are you sober now?"

"I wasn't drunk earlier. Just ill."

"I hope it's nothing deadly."

Saxon steps in front of her, blocking her view of the musician. "Can we cut the banter?"

The woman leans back in her chair to appraise him. "The direct approach. Sometimes it works."

"You weren't a dream."

"Not a very effective pick-up line."

"That's not a line. I've been having some very weird dreams lately."

The woman leans to see around Saxon. "She is very good. And I like this piece."

"de Falla's Spanish Dance Number One."

The woman glances back to Saxon to find him frowning at the young woman playing the harp. "You have better taste than you appear to have."

Saxon manages to force a smile. "Not a very effective pick-up line."

"No one is trying to pick you up. I am trying to enjoy the music."

"Should I leave?"

"That, or sit."

Saxon sits. The woman devotes her attention to the harpist. While Saxon tries his best to ignore the music that is obviously disturbing him. "Have you ever had a dream, then meet someone who was in that dream, someone you'd never seen before? At least you couldn't remember ever having seen that person before?"

"Are you referring to me? Am I in your weird dream?"

"Yes. If you could tell me why I'd certainly appreciate it."

"I'm no Freudian. If you want your dreams interpreted ..."

Saxon leans in close. "I want to know who I really am, why I'm here, and why I don't know these things."

The woman's bemused smile fades. "Amnesia? How clichéd."

Saxon leans back. "I haven't lost my memory. Just the opposite. I have too many of them. They are all jumbled up. Everything keeps changing." A waiter arrives with a wine glass for Saxon. They fall silent while he is present, the woman watching the harp player and Saxon looking away. He locates Obinna, who waves and smiles upon catching Saxon's eye. Saxon doesn't acknowledge him. He turns back to the woman seated across from him. She is filling the just-brought glass from her carafe. Saxon smiles his appreciation as she hands the glass of wine to him. "I'm sorry to bore you with this."

She fills her own glass. "No need to apologize. This is one of the more interesting conversations I've had since I've been here."

"Are you here alone?"

"No. I'm here with friends. And you're here with a Nigerian gentleman."

Saxon smiles. "So you *did* notice me. We're here to make a movie."

"You're an actor?"

"Stuntman. It's a football comedy. 'The World Cup Wonders'."

"I'll watch for it. How long are you staying in Prague?"

Saxon ponders before replying with hesitancy. "A day or two."

"So I'll see you around?"

Saxon breaks out his brightest smile. "Tomorrow? The café? Lunch?"

The woman nods, then directs her attention back to the harpist. "Please. I'd really like to hear her performance."

"Her Smetana piece, 'Vltave', is beautiful." When the woman's eyes follow him as he stands, Saxon explains. "I heard her practicing it this afternoon." He walks across the small restaurant to join Obinna at their table.

"She's beautiful. What's her name?"

Saxon halts halfway down into his chair. "I didn't ask."

Obinna laughs. "You really are addled."

Saxon settles down into his seat. "We have a lunch date for tomorrow. I'll ask her name then."

"Don't worry about her name. This afternoon I met a couple of women who'll make you forget all about her."

"It seems I can't forget about her." Saxon looks back to the woman. Her eyes are riveted on the harp player.

Obinna laughs at him. "It doesn't look like you really want to."

5

L ATER THAT NIGHT Saxon and Obinna walk into the small cellar cabaret Saxon had stuck his head into earlier. It is now well-lit and crowded. The two have shed their jackets and ties, and undone the top buttons of their shirts. Dark shadows and a haze of cigarette smoke obscure the Gothic architecture. On a tight corner stage, a young Czech beauty sings "Karma Chameleon", with a piano playing behind her. Obinna leads Saxon up to the bar and they put their drink orders in.

Obinna leans in to speak above the Culture Club song. "Their names are Hanako and Shino. They're here from Japan on vacation. First time in Prague. I met them at the cafe this afternoon. Told them we're in the business."

"Did you tell them we're stunt men?"

"Hey, if they mistake us for producers, it's not our fault. There they are." Obinna points out two oriental dazzlers in club dresses walking in the door. "Hanako's mine." He leads the way to the pair standing just inside the door. "I hope you had a good dinner."

"Did you enjoy the harp music?" Saxon asks.

Both smile without smiling, glance at Obinna with concern.

"At the restaurant," Obinna attempts to clarify.

"We didn't eat here," one of them replies.

"We went exploring," the other offers. "Got totally lost in these mad little alleys."

"Ended up eating some bread rolls dipped in cheese," the tag team continued.

"A street vendor was selling them."

"Rohilky," Saxon states.

The two women fall silent and, along with Obinna, stare expectantly at Saxon, who seems as surprised as they that he knows what they are talking about.

"You've had them?" one of the Japanese ladies asks. "They're good, aren't they?"

"I … I don't know."

Obinna lunges in to cover his confusion. "We had beef gulas with dumplings, at the inn."

"Knedliky." Following more blank stares from the other three, Saxon wades on. "The dumplings. They're called *knedliky*."

Obinna smiles, with just a hint of irritation, then turns back to the women. "What would you like to drink?"

Both of them look to Saxon, and one speaks up. "What do you suggest?"

"Velkopopovicky Kozel," Saxon replies without hesitation. "If you like beer. Czech beer is the best in the world." Both women nod agreeably.

"Then it's all around? I'll go get it. If I can pronounce it." Obinna departs for the bar, but doesn't get far. He darts back. "Forgive my poor manners. Ladies, this is Saxon. Saxon, Hanako and Shino." Each nods at the mention of their name. Obinna departs for the bar once again.

"You should be commended," Hanako says, in a tone that doesn't sound commendable. "To have committed the guide book to memory."

Saxon twitches a smile. "I haven't, really. I just seem to be chock full of useless information. By the way, we're stuntmen. Just wanted to get that straight. Ben is prone to exaggerate."

"Is that how you hurt your head?"

•   •   •

Saxon, in rags, beaten and bloody, lies in a heap on the bare ground looking up as a rifle butt stabs down from above to bash him in the head.

•   •   •

Saxon is staggered by the memory. Shino reaches out a steadying hand.

While Hanako is less sympathetic. "Maybe the Czech beer is *too* good."

Saxon regains his balance, smiles his appreciation at Shino. He touches the lump on his forehead. "I forgot that it was there. The rest was just makeup. They weren't real. They didn't hurt. I cleaned them off. But this one *is* real."

Obinna rejoins them with a tray of beer bottles and glasses. He frowns at Saxon. "What did I miss?"

"He just got dizzy," Shino offered. "That's a bad lump on his head."

Obinna tries to laugh it off. "Yeah. Boz gave that to him."

"Bozidar?" Hanako seems impressed. "The football player?"

"Is he in your movie?" Shino asks, tightening her grip on Saxon's arm.

"Yes. Saxon here forgot Bozidar is not an actor. Boz is the real deal."

Saxon pats the lump. "We were staging a stunt."

"Have you worked in any movies we might have seen?" Shino asks.

Saxon frowns, trying to remember. "I don't know."

"He is in 'The Caves of Kandahar'," Obinna covers. "But that hasn't been released yet. I was in 'Full Throttle'."

"Is that a racing movie?" Hanako asks.

"No. It's about a strangler." Obinna frowns at Shino's laugh. "It isn't a comedy. It's pretty intense." He turns to Hanako. "Let's dance."

"What about our drinks?"

"I'll hold them," Saxon offers. He offers Shino an apology with his eyes. "I don't think I'm up to dancing."

Obinna hands him the tray. "Drink a couple of these and you'll be fine." He leads Hanako away.

"We need to find a table." Shino, still holding his arm, leads him through the mob.

6

L ATER THAT NIGHT, Saxon and Shino stroll along the river on a cobblestone lane. The way is well-lit, but fog from the river is heavy. It is late, and not many others are out. Shino holds his arm as they walk. "Sorry I turned out to be such a dud," he apologizes.

Shino smiles up at him. "At least you tried to dance. You just got dizzy."

"Fresh air is helping."

"For me, too. I don't like crowds. This is much better." They walk a while without speaking. They are blanketed in silence, the dense fog buffering all sights and sounds of the city. "So you are having a hard time remembering things?"

"Some things. Other things just pop into my head. Like earlier, about the food and beer. And this music I don't like that I keep hearing everywhere. And how I got hit in the head. I'm not sure it was from doing a stunt. I remember getting hit in the head another way. But then it could be from colliding with Bozidar. I remember that happening, too. Some things I remember turn out not to be true. Like earlier today I believed I was a real football player."

"Instead of a stunt man pretending to be one?"

"Not pretending. Acting."

"That must be exciting. You must get to meet some famous stars."

"Yes, and I hope to soon remember who they were."

Shino laughs then chokes it back. "I'm sorry. It's not funny."

Saxon smiles to relieve her discomfort. "Ben tells me I'm improving."

"So what's the last thing you remember?"

•   •   •

Saxon and Shino are in bed in the dark, the clothes they are presently wearing scattered all across the room.

•   •   •

"Saxon?" Shino's breathless voice brings him back to the present.

Saxon takes a deep calming breath to steady himself. He then is able to focus on Shino's worried expression. She is staring beyond him. He glances casually over his shoulder to find three young men approach out of the fog. The ominous trio halts several paces away.Saxon turns to greet them in a casual tone."Hello."

"You know Czech," one young tough remarks. "That makes this easier. Hand over your wallet." He glances to Shino. "And her dress." The other two begin to encircle them. "She better not scream." He produces a knife. "We'll have your throats cut and your bodies in the river before anyone can find you in this fog."

Saxon drops into a fighting crouch.

The young tough smiles, glancing at his two companions. "Looks like we have a hero." He advances, waving the knife, while the other two hang back.

Saxon disarms him by snapping his wrist. While he sinks to his knees shrieking, the other two charge. Saxon sidesteps one. The other he hurls into the river. Saxon spins just in time to see the one he had dodged produce a knife. Saxon kicks it out of his hand. Disarmed, he flees into the fog. Saxon spins to find the first young tough rising to his feet. Holding his injured wrist, he, too, turns and runs away into the fog.

"Come on, Saxon!"

Saxon turns to find Shino had run off and nearly disappeared into the fog herself. He joins her, and they run away.

Reaching a main street where other people are around, she collapses into his arms. She is trembling. "I'm sorry. In the daytime these alleys seemed harmless. Please take me back to my room. That was way too scary." Saxon nods. He looks back over his shoulder. No one is following them.

Shino hugs him as they walk. She places a hand on his chest. "You're a cool one. It's not even beating fast." She places his hand over her heart. "Feel that? That's what fear feels like." Shino continues to hold his hand to her breast as she lays her head on his shoulder and hugs him close while walking.

Shino's room proves to be similar to Saxon's. She heads straight for the liquor on her dresser. "I need a drink. Badly. What would you like?"

Saxon closes and locks the door. "An ale. But I'll take a shot of whiskey." When she offers it to him, he sees her hand shaking. He takes it, then steps up to the dresser. "Let me. What would you like?"

Shino smiles gratefully. "Whiskey and cola on ice. With very little cola or ice."

Saxon mixes her drink. When he turns back around he finds her sitting hugged up into a ball in a chair next to the bed. He walks over to serve her drink. She unballs one arm to accept it, looking up with a dark complexion at him. Saxon takes a step back. "Maybe I should go."

"Please don't." Shino motions the bed. Saxon sits on the edge, facing her. "How did you learn to fight like that? From doing stunts?"

Saxon takes a sip of his drink to give himself time to consider. "I guess. To be able to fake a fight convincingly you would have to learn the real moves."

"Why did he scream?"

"I broke his wrist."

"Good." Shino gulps down the rest of her drink.

"Would you like another?"

"Yesterday."

Saxon takes her glass to the dresser and mixes another whiskey and cola. Turning back with it in hand, he finds Shino stepping out of her dress. In a sexy panty and bra set, she drapes the dress over the back of the chair. "I have never been so scared in my life. Thank you." She steps up to embrace Saxon and lay her head on his chest.

"You already thanked me."

"That was just the preliminaries." Shino begins unbuttoning his shirt.

"What about Hanako?"

"She won't be back. She has plans for the night. With Ben."

"He doesn't like being called that."

"I don't think he'll care what Hanako calls him." Shino pulls his shirt open. She traces some old scars with her fingers. "Stunt work must be dangerous."

"I had a lot more scars earlier today."

"You must heal fast." She begins undoing his pants. "Any scars down here?"

"I don't know. I haven't looked that closely."

"I'll let you know." She pulls his pants down. She rises and urges him to sit down on the edge of the bed once more. "I'll take these." She takes her drink and downs it. Then she downs what's left of his.

Saxon laughs. "Keep drinking like that and I'll be tucking you into bed."

Shino sets both empty glasses down on the nightstand. "You'll be doing *what* to me in bed?"

"Tucking you in. Tucking. I said tucking."

"I heard something else." She removes his shoes and socks. Shino drops them on the floor then removes his pants, also. Crawling on top of Saxon, forcing him flat onto his back. They kiss passionately.

•　　•　　•

Saxon, naked flat on his back in bed, looks up at the Russian woman, also naked, astride his hips leering down at him.

•　　•　　•

Saxon is shocked into inaction.

Seeing this, Shino pauses, too. "Is something wrong?"

He manages to smile up at her. He is getting used to these vivid flashbacks. "Nothing. So long as you don't mind us having a *ménage a trois.*"

Shino looks around the room. "Is someone here I don't know about?"

Saxon points to his head. "There's a crowd of strange people in here."

Shino removes her bra. "I'll make you forget about everyone in there but me." She loops the garment around his wrists and ties it loosely.

•　　•　　•

Saxon is lying naked on a bed face up, with the Russian woman sitting naked astride him, same as before. Only now Saxon's hands can be seen to be tied to the headboard, and the Russian is smoking. Inhaling deeply, she brings the tip to a bright red glow. She ever so slowly lowers it to his chest. As his skin sizzles, he screams in agony, thrashing about while pulling hard on the ropes binding his hands.

•   •   •

Saxon yanks his hands free of the bra. Shino stares in wonder at his terrified face. He tosses the bra aside, struggling to compose himself. "Let's don't do that. I like for my hands to be free." He grabs both breasts with both hands and pulls her down to him. Then he reaches around to slip both hands inside her panties and grasp her bottom.

Shino laughs. "By all means, use your hands." Their lovemaking turns silent and serious.

7

S AXON, STRIPPED TO HIS UNDERSHORTS, lies in a listless heap in a small steel cage while a violin concerto blares. He has a blood-soaked bandage across his stomach, a gunshot wound that has been treated with only minimal care. He is filthy, and appears to be in much pain.

He looks around. There are five other men like him in small steel cages, stripped to their undershorts, wounded and dirty. Gathered around the cages are several ragged well-armed bearded men standing guard.

The guards all look off. Someone is coming. Saxon follows their line of sight. An elderly man in a clean white lab coat approaches, followed by an assistant carrying a video camera. The Doctor speaks to one of the guards. He and another go to a cage, open it, and drag a wounded man out. The man screams in pain as he is drug across the floor by the arms.

Saxon yells, objecting to the way the man is being treated. The guards ignore him. But the Doctor turns to stare. Saxon and he lock eyes.

• • •

Saxon opens his eyes with a start, the wounded man's screams of pain and the orchestral music echoing in his head. He looks all around, upset by the dream, to find himself alone in bed. It is broad daylight. He sees his clothes are strewn across the floor, Shino's dress draped across the back of the chair. Reaching under the covers, he pulls out her panties. Finally remembering where he is, in Shino's bed, in her and Hanako's room, in Prague, he smiles contentedly. He looks toward the bathroom, where he hears water from the shower running.

Saxon stretches every part of his body that will stretch, then tosses back the covers. He is naked. He sits up on the edge of the bed. He finds his undershorts on the floor, next to Shino's bra.

• • •

Saxon, in his shirt and undershorts, is flat on his back on the bed with Shino sitting astride his hips in her matching panty and bra. She removes her bra and loops it around his wrists.

• • •

It is a pleasant memory for a change, and Saxon smiles. He leans over to pick up his undershorts then pulls them up his legs. He stands to pull them the rest of the way up.

Saxon starts toward the bathroom, but his foot kicks something. He looks down to see a book splayed open on the floor, as if he had fallen asleep reading it. He stoops to pick it up. 'The Metamorphosis', by Franz Kafka. He quickly flips it to the first page inside the cover. The smashed bug is there.

Suddenly apprehensive, Saxon slaps the book shut and sets it down on the nightstand and hurries into the bathroom. Shino is in the shower. Saxon studies her shadowy form behind the shower curtain. Finally, he pulls the curtain back

A Latino woman lathered up in soap stands naked before him. She greets him with a smile, and in Spanish. "Good morning, Sajon."

"Who are you?!" Saxon yells.

The woman exhales a deep world-weary sigh. "Back to speaking English?" she asks in heavily-accented English. "And I thought we were making progress."

Saxon runs out of the bathroom. Snatches his pants up from the floor and digs through the pockets. Pulls out a slip of paper. Unfolds it and looks. The number nine, scribbled in his handwriting. Saxon drops the pants and rushes to the door, unlocks it, and yanks it open. Looks at the room number. Nine. Shaking his head, he closes the door and wads the paper up, tossing it down on the floor.

The woman calls out to him from the bathroom. "We went for a walk along the river last night. I hope you remember *that*."

•   •   •

On the cobblestone lane along the river at night, Saxon, wearing the clothes from the night before, walks hand in hand with the woman in the shower, who is wearing the same club dress Shino had been wearing.

•   •   •

The voice from the bathroom continues. "It was very romantic."

Saxon rushes to the chair and snatches up the dress. It is identical to what Shino had worn. He tosses it aside then rushes to the wardrobe and throws it open. Inside are female clothes along with the male clothes he has become familiar with. Saxon rushes back into the bathroom. "Valeria?"

"You *do* remember."

"Where's Shino?"

Valeria's head emerges from behind the shower curtain. "She who?"

"The woman I was with last night."

Her head withdraws back behind the curtain. "If you are dreaming about other women I don't want to hear about it."

"Were we attacked? Last night? By the river?"

"I was attacked. It was wonderful."

•　　　•　　　•

Up against a building along the river, at night, in the fog, their clothes half-off, Saxon and Valeria make love.

•　　　•　　　•

Saxon staggers back out of the bathroom. He stumbles about gathering up his clothes and begins yanking them on.

The water in the shower stops. "Sajon? Are you okay?"

"This is like the damn Body Snatchers! Fall asleep and you wake up as someone else!"

"Honey! You had a bad head injury."

Half-dressed, Saxon charges into the bathroom. Valeria now stands outside the shower drying off with a towel. "Who the hell are you!?"

"Your wife! Now settle down."

Saxon's glare drips venom as he watches her dry herself. "You are not my wife."

Saxon spins on heel and rushes out. He jams his feet into a pair of shoes. Dashes over to the night stand and yanks the drawer open. Scoops up change, his wallet. He stuffs these articles into his pockets then roots through the drawer, searching for something else.

Valeria walks out of the bathroom with a towel wrapped around her. "What are you doing?"

"Where is my passport?"

"It's not there?"

Saxon lunges at her. "Where is it!?"

"I don't know! You've lost it? I was supposed to keep it for you, since your injury. But you wouldn't let me. Now it's gone? We'll have to contact the Colombian embassy."

"Why would I contact the Colombian embassy?"

"Because you have a Colombian passport." She opens her arms to hug and comfort him.

Saxon is having none of it. He shoves her aside and dashes for the door.

Valeria is frantic. "Sajon! We'll get it later! You have to calm down!"

Saxon throws the door open then looks back at her. "How can I calm down? Every time I fall asleep I wake up a different person." He advances on her, leaving the door wide open. Valeria backs away fearfully, but he lunges forward and grabs her arms, shaking her. "What am I today? A stunt man? A football player?"

Valeria goes limp in his arms as she begins to cry. The towel is shaken loose and slides down her body to the floor. "You're a construction worker."

·　　　·　　　·

At a construction site, Saxon, in work clothes and hard hat (one that resembles an Army helmet), walks a metal beam on the third floor of an office building that is going up. In the distance can be seen Prague Castle across the Vltava River.

·　　　·　　　·

"Yeah? So what happened to me? This time?"

"You were at a football game. At the stadium. Sinobo. You and a bunch of your co-workers went to see the Czechs play the English. You had too much to drink. As usual. And you fell and hit your head."

·　　　·　　　·

Saxon lies flat on his back on the concrete steps of an upper level of the stadium. Huddled around and staring down at him with grave concern are Philip, Obinna, and Bozidar.

•   •   •

"You've had a bad concussion. You've been out of your head since yesterday. I thought you were getting better, Sajon."

"Better? You bet I'm better." Saxon shoves Valeria down onto the bed and bolts for the door.

"Sajon! Wait!"

Saxon spins to face her in the open door.

Valeria sits up in bed, pulling the covers up around her. "What's the last thing you remember?"

Saxon glares at her in disbelief.

"Never mind. Just come back in and close the door. Please, Sajon. Don't stand there with the door open. I'm naked." Valeria lets the covers fall away.

Saxon laughs. "Nice try, bitch." He runs out, leaving the door open.

Saxon hurries down the stairs to the lobby and up to the front desk. The same clerk as before is there. The clerk looks up coolly at his manic approach.

"I've lost my passport."

"Name?"

"Saxon Hedges. I think. I've been called Sajon."

"Yes. Sajon is Spanish for Saxon. Room?"

"I have no idea. I'm all over the place."

The desk clerk gives a calm sigh. "Identification?"

"I sure hope so." Saxon digs his wallet out and rifles through it. Pulling out an ID card, he starts to hand it over. Until he glances at it. As the clerk reaches out his hand, Saxon yanks the card back and stares at it. His photo is on it. With the name Sajon Hedges, with his country of origin as Columbia, and a Cali address.

The clerk leans over to look at it. He smiles. "You're in luck, Senor Hedges." He produces a passport and compares it to Saxon's face and the photo on the ID card. "It was found last night in the cabaret." He hands it to Saxon.

Saxon inspects the passport. It has been issued by Columbia. He slowly flips through it. The stamps are the same as before, except now there is a stamp from Great Britain. Saxon stares at the British stamp in amazement.

"You should be more careful with your passport."

Saxon stuffs the wallet back into his pants pocket, but continues to look the passport over. "Thank you."

"Gracias, señor."

Saxon looks up to find the desk clerk mocking his confusion. He wanders away across the lobby, still looking the passport over.

The same female tour operator as before sits at the same desk. She stands as Saxon wanders by. "Mister Hedges?" She holds a ticket out to him. "Your bus is ready to leave."

Saxon glances out the front entrance to the lobby. A tour bus is loading before the inn. He looks back to the tour operator. "I didn't buy a tour."

She waves the ticket. "You really need to go on this tour. Many questions will be answered."

Valeria dashes down the stairs into the lobby. She has thrown on some clothes without touching her wet hair. "Sajon!"

Saxon snatches the ticket and turns toward the door.

Valeria runs up to him. "What are you doing?"

"Going on a tour." He walks out the door.

Valeria is on his heels. "Where to?"

"I have no idea." He hands the ticket to the tour guide standing at the open bus door.

The tour guide has overheard their exchange. "The Philosopher's Walk, at Kutna Hora."

Saxon smiles pleasantly at him then starts to board.

Valeria grabs Saxon. "I'm going, too."

"Sorry," the tour guide informs her. "The tour is full."

"You don't understand," Valeria insists. "My husband is not well. He can't go off on his own."

Saxon makes his smile even more pleasant. "I'm not her husband. She is the one not well. Just look at her." He knocks her hands off.

Undeniably, Valeria is a mess. She steps back. "What am I going to do all day?"

"Whatever it was you did yesterday. Before I ever laid eyes on you."

The tour guide smiles at Valeria's distress. "We'll take good care of him." He steps onto the bus and closes the door in her face.

As the driver settles in behind the wheel, Saxon walks down the aisle. He looks out the window. Valeria stands at the curb, distraught, staring up at the tinted windows of the bus without being able to see through them.

The tour guide calls out from the front. "You need to take a seat, sir."

Saxon nods as he looks around. He spies one unoccupied seat, an aisle seat next to a young woman staring out the window. "Miss, do you mind if I sit here?" When she turns around he sees it is the Russian. Surprise registers as he sits. "You're a sight for sore eyes."

She shakes her head. "Another lame pick up line."

"Do you know what's going on?"

The woman looks around. "We can't talk now. You never know who is listening." She looks back to Saxon. "Once we get off at Kutna Hora we can go off by ourselves."

Saxon looks around the bus. The passengers are a varied collection of mostly European tourists. None seem to be paying any special attention to him. But then there are a few curious stares. So he looks back to the woman, nodding agreement. And smiles. Encountering this one constant of the last several days has had a calming effect. "By the way, my name is Saxon. Or Sajon."

The woman speaks while gazing out the window. "It's Saxon. Your wife looked quite upset. A bad night?"

"A bad morning. The night was exceptional."

She looks back out the window. "I'm sure it was. I saw you with that Oriental beauty in the cabaret last night."

"So it wasn't a dream."

"Not unless I was having the same dream. So, how is the stunt man this morning? Are you healing?"

"I'm no longer a stunt man. That was so yesterday."

"So what are you today?"

"A construction worker."

"Really?" She takes his hands in hers and turns them over, inspecting. "Shouldn't your hands be more calloused?" She releases them. "I don't believe you do much work with your hands."

"How about play football? That's what I was doing yesterday morning."

"Who did you play for?"

Saxon is surprised, as he considers. "I don't know. I should know. Shouldn't I?"

He begins growing agitated, shifting about in his seat and glancing around at the other passengers, who now, in this mood, seem to be piercing him with evil eyes. The Russian woman takes his hand and squeezes it to reassure him. Saxon gives her a black glare. She in return gives him a slight smile. With a struggle, Saxon takes a deep settling breath. He squeezes her hand in return; he is not about to let go of it. "What do you think? Do I play for an English team or a Colombian team?"

"You don't look Latino to me."

"I thought that, too."

"But then some Latinos don't look Latino. Can you speak the language?"

Without hesitation, Saxon answers in Spanish. "Yes, I can." He continues in Czech. "My Czech is quite good, too."

"How about Russian?"

"Of course," Saxon answers in Russian. He taps his head. "I wonder what other languages are hiding in there, just waiting to pop out?"

"What's your native tongue?"

Saxon considers, to no avail. "I wish I knew. Just one more question. Who are you? Why are you helping me? What …"

"My name is Irina. Please wait until we can be alone before asking any more questions." Irina looks out the window.

Saxon scoots down in his seat so he can look over her shoulder out the window at the passing Prague scenery. They have passed out of Old Town into a more modern neighborhood, He continues to grip her hand, while her fingers work to reassure his. After a short while his eyes begin to droop.

8

*S*AXON, CLAD IN DESERT CAMOUFLAGE *and with his face streaked with camouflage paint, with a full backpack, a helmet on his head, and an automatic rifle on his lap, sits in the back of a truck in the dark with a dozen other similarly outfitted men. He seems relaxed, head back with eyes closed. He could be napping, even though the ride is bumpy, jostling him. The truck hits something big or deep, and gives a jarring jolt.*

•   •   •

Saxon jerks awake with teeth rattling. He sits straight up, peers all around in a panic. There is no truck, no other soldiers, it is not night. He is on a crowded bus filled with tourists, in the daylight.

"We hit a bump." He jerks around to find Irina seated next to him. "These country roads aren't the best."

Saxon takes a deep breath and gazes out the window. They are out of the city and traveling through a forest. In the trees near the road he sees peasants bent over gathering something from the ground. "What are they doing?"

"Picking mushrooms. These woods are filled with large ones. Every fall the peasants harvest them."

Saxon leans back in his seat, watching the many peasants gathering mushrooms in the deep medieval woods passing by. At last, his racing heart slows. He looks back to Irina. He hopes it is still Irina. "Irina?"

She smiles. "Yes. You dozed off. Did you wake up from a bad dream?"

"Yes." Saxon patiently waits. Finally, "Aren't you going to ask me?"

"Ask you what?"

"What everybody else asks me." Getting only a mystified look, Saxon dismisses the notion. "Never mind." He looks out the window. They are emerging from the forest into the fringes of a city. "Where are we?"

"Kutna Hora."

The bus passes from the contemporary into the historic district, which resembles a small medieval town laid out on hillsides above a dense fairy-tale like Bohemian woods. Above cobble streets and colonnades stand the brightly-colored and carved facades of patrician houses. Dominating the town from high above is the Gothic cathedral of Santa Barbara, its three towers topped with golden balls rising in graceful curves. Caught up in his surroundings, Saxon holds his tongue, content to gaze out at the passing scenery. Until the tour bus pulls up before an open plaza.

"First stop on the tour," Irina announces. "The Museum Alchemy."

People stand and line up to file out of the bus. Once Saxon and Irina emerge, she searches all around. In the distance are several groups of people wandering through the old town. Saxon notices her concern. "What is it?"

"There are other tour groups here. Buses are slow. Once they learned where we were taking you they could have sped some people up here to mix in with other groups."

Saxon looks all around, too. But in the shifting shadows of an overcast morning it is difficult to make out details. "Who are *they*?"

"Your keepers." The group Saxon and Irina are with move *en masse* toward the entrance to the Alchemy Museum. The two fall in with them.

The tour group walks through massive wooden doors down a stone corridor where framed illustrations from old alchemy books hang on the walls. They pass by a large Golem and on to a chapel table, upon which are displayed lit candles, a quill and inkwell, a first edition of a medieval alchemy book, a human skull, and a small, shriveled crocodile. Unlike the others, Saxon pays scant attention to these items, or to any of his surroundings. He concentrates on Irina, who at least attempts to appear to be an interested tourist. He bends down to whisper in her ear. "I was told that many questions would be answered on this tour."

"So ask."

"Who am I?"

"Saxon Hedges."

"So the name is real."

"As far as I know."

"Who are my keepers? Why are they keeping me? And who are you and why are you answering my questions?"

"Saxon, slow down. And look around some. You are supposed to be a tourist."

Saxon takes a deep breath and gazes around. They descend a stone spiral staircase that winds down into the musty darkness of a basement laboratory. Here, a massive bellows bathed in artificial light from a nearby fireplace dominates the room. Shelves crowded with reproductions of clay pots and vessels shaped like different animals. Glowing glass cases filled with odd-sized bottles with murky indeterminable contents. But Saxon has held his tongue as long as he can. He leans in close to rasp into Irina's ear. "Why should I believe what you say? Everything I've heard here has been lies."

Irina takes Saxon by the arm and leads him off to the side. "Please be quieter. I'm sure they have some people here. Like at the inn."

"What do you mean?"

"Most of the people at the inn are just tourists or employees. But some are their people. A few are ours."

"The desk clerk?"

"Theirs."

"The tour operator? The woman who gave me the ticket?"

"Ours."

"My so-called wife?"

"Theirs, of course."

By this time Saxon and Irina have followed their group to an ornate metal door set in stone. One by one the tourists step up to peer through a tiny window in the door. Saxon grows apprehensive as they approach.

Irina notices his nervousness. "What's wrong?"

Saxon shakes his head, releases her hand. He begins to tremble, to sweat. With each step he grows more desperate.

Irina watches him, but says no more.

At last, it is Saxon's turn to step up to the window. Grabbing the wall to steady himself, gulping down a deep breath and holding it, holding his heartbeat, he peers inside. He sees a recreation of a tiny cell holding the haggard remains of a wizened alchemist who died while stubbornly refusing to reveal his secret formula to his patron.

·　　·　　·

Saxon, inside the cell, stares back out at himself. He is naked, beaten and bloody and filthy, deranged beyond all hope. He holds out his trembling clenched fist. Unfolds his trembling fingers. Inside is a cockroach. As it starts to scurry away to freedom, Saxon clamps his fist closed again. Its shell pops. Greenish juices run out between his clenched fingers. Saxon opens his fist again, presenting the Saxon gazing into the cell with the smashed bug. It looks just like the smashed bug inside the copy of "The Metamorphosis" he has. Saxon stuffs the crushed cockroach into his mouth and chews it up and swallows it, afterwards licking the juices that had run out of his hand down his arm. Looking up as he licks, he smiles, displaying his insanity.

•   •   •

Saxon screams, jumps back from the door.

Irina catches him, as everyone in the room turns toward his scream. "What is it, Saxon? What did you see?"

Saxon jerks all about, away from Irina, trying to flee. "Me! In there! Looking out at me!"

"What were you doing? What was going on in there?"

"I had a bug. A cockroach. I crushed it. Then I ate it."

The other members of the group back away to a safe distance, watching.

Irina ignores them. "That's not so unusual. For someone starving. To eat a bug."

"I didn't look starved. I looked half-dead. More than half crazy. But not starved." Saxon's trembling eases, his wild manic expression softens, as he begins to recover from the vision. "Why would I eat a bug?"

Irina's glare is fierce, but she says nothing else.

Until the tour guide joins them. "What is wrong?"

"Something down here has made him ill. We'll go outside and wait for you." Irina supports a shaky Saxon across the room back to the spiral staircase. Under the tour guide's scrutiny.

Irina and Saxon emerge from the Museum Alchemy and walk off the plaza onto a side street. They pass alcoves cut into stone walls where silversmiths worked in the Middle Ages minting coins.

Other groups of tourists are in sight in the distance. Saxon seems somewhat recovered, but still shaky. "Why am I so important?"

"You know something, Saxon."

"What?"

"I don't know what. You'll have to tell me what."

He grabs Irina by the shoulders. "I'm sick of these games!"

"Saxon. Please. Don't attract any more attention."

A local police officer looms up behind them. "Is there a problem?"

"No. No problem. My husband and I are just discussing something personal."

He looks them over. "Are you with a tour group?"

"Yes." Irina points back toward the plaza. Their group is just emerging from the Museum Alchemy.

The officer sees where she is pointing. "I suggest you rejoin them. So you don't get left behind."

Irina escorts a still-stumbling Saxon back onto the plaza. As they arrive at the bus, the tour guide greets her. "Is he feeling better?"

"Yes." Irina mangles her attempt at a smile.

"Good. Kutna Hora has many charms. The Philosopher's Walk has much more to offer."

Saxon, at last, releases Irina's arms. Boarding the bus, she doesn't even glance at the handprints from his fierce grip which are forming bruises. Saxon pauses at the open door to look down the several side streets branching off the plaza. He has no idea where he is, no idea of how to get to somewhere he does know. Having no other option, he steps up onto the bus. He takes the seat next to Irina. As the bus pulls away from the curb she ignores him, staring out the window, while Saxon stares only at her.

They tour their next destination, Santa Barbara Cathedral, in silence and without incident. Emerging, they cross a ridge-top stone bridge lined with baroque statues. Saxon leans down to speak into Irina's ear. "That damn guide won't leave us alone for a second now."

"We'll get away at Sedlec."

"What is Sedlec?"

"The last stop on our tour. It's smaller and won't be as crowded." As they arrive at the bus, a different driver awaits them at the door. Irina is concerned. "Where's our driver?"

"He became ill. I'll finish driving this tour."

As Saxon and Irina board, he whispers, "One of theirs?"

Irina nods. They pass in solemn silence down the aisle back to their seats. As they sit she looks out the window. Her reflection in the glass appears distressed.

"Is it that bad?"

Irina nods.

"Can't we talk?"

She shoots him a sharp look, shaking her head no. She scans the people boarding. "A lot of these people are different."

Saxon looks around. He sees there are many who weren't with their original tour group. "Are we on the wrong bus?"

Irina shakes her head no as she gazes back out the window.

Saxon stares at her. He reaches for her hand.

Irina glances back at Saxon. She smiles nervously and squeezes his hand.

While Saxon continues to gaze only at her.

9

S AXON AND IRINA step down out of the tour bus. They are at a small medieval church. Saxon looks all around anxiously. He is becoming upset, as he had in the Museum Alchemy. "What is this place?" Saxon steps away, gazing into the adjoining graveyard.

•   •   •

Dead naked male bodies piled tightly together, much like the tombstones in the Old Jewish Cemetery, their faces locked in rictal agony and covered in dried blood that had streamed from their mouths, ears, eyes, noses. Elsewhere, dried blood is all around their groins and their buttocks, from where it had flowed profusely from those orifices. And the demonic violin plays.

•   •   •

Saxon staggers back into Irina's arms. "What is it? What do you see?"

Saxon jerks free and turns on her. "Why do you keep asking me that!? What do I see!? What's the last thing I remember!? Why does everybody want to know what I remember!?"

"Is he ill again?" The tour guide has found them again.

Irina attempts a smile. "I apologize for being such a problem."

Their benevolent tour guide smiles. "You are no problem. Many tourists come to Prague and get sick. They enjoy our fine Czech beer so much they don't know when to stop enjoying it." He urges them toward the graveyard, where the rest of the group awaits. The people part to make room for the pair.

Saxon looks about with a scowl as they proceed, feeling like a herded sheep. They are soon trapped in the middle of the group. Irina attempts to squeeze his hand to reassure him, but he shakes his hand free.

The tour guide steps to the front to address the entire group. "In twelve seventy-eight an abbot from this Cistercian chapel embarked on a pilgrimage to the Holy Land. While in Palestine he visited the Golgotha, and from there brought back to Sedlec a jar of earth, which he spread over this cemetery."

The tour guide waves his arm at the cemetery. "Because of that, this cemetery soon became thought of as very sacred land. It rapidly became one of the most popular cemeteries in central Europe. People from all over Europe brought their dead here for burial. Many corpses were accumulated this way, especially during the times of the Black Plague. By thirteen eighteen over thirty thousand bodies were buried here. This gave rise to the creation of the ossuary."

The tour guide turns away from the graveyard and leads the way toward the church. "All Saints' Chapel, which houses the ossuary, was built about fourteen hundred. The ossuary itself dates from fifteen eleven, when a half-blind monk was given the task to gather the bones from the abolished graves and put them in the crypt to make room for new customers. With so many coming here to be buried, and limited space, this was necessary."

The tour guide stops at the entrance to the chapel, and the group gathers before him. "By eighteen seventy the bones of over forty thousand bodies were in storage. So a local woodcarver was hired to take advantage of this abundance. Frantisek Rindt was employed by the Duke of Swartzenberg to design the magnificent objects you are about to see with the plentiful supply of human bones at his disposal."

The tour guide opens the doors wide and leads the group inside. Saxon stares fearfully into the church, with Irina clinging to him, as the rest of the group streams past to enter. Irina tries to pull Saxon away. But he shrugs her off and, steeling himself for the ordeal ahead, forces himself to enter. Irina follows in on his heels.

Inside All Saints Chapel, the tour guide continues his spiel. "Such as the Shwartzenberg family coat of arms. And the chandelier, which contains every bone in the human body, several times over." As he speaks, these items — the coat of arms, the chandelier, and others — come into view. All constructed of human bones. The walls are lined with human skulls and bones arranged in exotic designs. Perched upon ledges along the ceiling human skulls stare down at the tourists. Strands of human skulls drape down from the ceiling in long dangling loops. Carefully arranged piles of human skulls and bones form obelisks. An anchor constructed of human bones hangs on the wall. The artist's signature in human bones, too, is on the wall.

Saxon stares all around in wonder as he stumbles about. He seems to be in a daze.

Irina holds him by the arm, guiding him. Ignoring the bones, she has eyes only for Saxon.

•   •   •

Saxon and several other wounded filthy men, all stripped to their undershorts, are in small individual steel cages. While violin music fills the air, many well-armed raggedly-dressed bearded men stand about the cages watching. One wounded man is strapped to a table. The Doctor and an assistant with a video camera approach the table.

•　　　•　　　•

Saxon staggers over to gaze up at the chandelier.

•　　　•　　　•

The Doctor, humming the violin music, approaches the table with a needle. The assistant films the procedure. The Doctor injects something into the strapped-down man. He steps back to watch. The man, thinking he is at last receiving medical treatment for his wounds, smiles hopefully up at the Doctor.

•　　　•　　　•

Saxon staggers up to the coat of arms fashioned out of human bones.

•　　　•　　　•

The strapped-down man begins to sweat. Badly. Then he contorts into a knot, as if he is having severe cramps. His body convulses. Blood oozes from every opening — his mouth, his nose, his ears, his eyes — just like the bodies Saxon has been seeing piled on top of each other. Blood stains the front of his undershorts, blood pools beneath his hips. He thrashes about screaming in agony. Until he grows still. He is dead.

•　　　•　　　•

Saxon stumbles over to the anchor fashioned of human bones.

•　　　•　　　•

Still humming, the Doctor notes the time on a chart, then checks with his assistant to make sure he has filmed it all. The medical table is wheeled out by several of the armed men standing about watching. The Doctor and his assistant with the camera walk out, conferring dispassionately as they go.

•   •   •

Saxon barges all about the large room. Irina holds him by the arm, trying to guide him forward, to see more, to see all of the human bones. Until they arrive before the pyramid. A hut-like structure, built of thousands and thousands of human bones, its walls thick with bones. There is a small entrance. Saxon shuffles unsteadily toward the entrance, aided by Irina. He moves up close, to peer into the cave-like structure.

•   •   •

Saxon is now strapped to a similar table, with the Doctor and the assistant with the camera and several armed men gathered around. Of course the violin music is there to serenade him, which the Doctor hums along with. Saxon watches in tense fear as the Doctor injects a needle into his arm. A brief moment later Saxon SCREAMS!!

•   •   •

When Saxon opens his eyes, Irina's serene face fills his vision. "What happened?"

"You passed out."

"I was somewhere. Else." Saxon realizes he is on his back on the bare ground. He tries to rise up.

Irina prevents this. "Relax. Rest. You need to recover."

Saxon lays back, looks around. He is lying on the grass outside the church, with Irina kneeling beside him. He looks back to Irina, as confused as ever. "People were dying. Horrible deaths. An old man. A doctor. Was killing them. With something he injected them with. He injected me."

"But you didn't die."

"Why? Why didn't I die? Like the rest?" Saxon struggles to sit up once again.

This time Irina helps him. He pierces her eyes with his bewildered fury. "This is why you brought me here. To make me remember. Something horrible. Something I don't want to remember. And to tell you about it."

"I brought you here to get you away from them."

"You want to know what I see. You're no different from the others."

"I am, Saxon! I care about you!" Irina throws herself on him, embracing him. As they fall back to the ground she tries to kiss him.

• • •

Saxon and a dark-haired female, both naked, are in bed engaged in violent sex, with her on top. Saxon jerks and thrashes beneath her, same as he had while being shocked. With a laugh, the woman tosses her hair back, revealing her face. It is Irina.

• • •

Saxon shoves her away. "Don't kiss me."

"Why?"

"I don't know why. Just don't." Irina settles comfortably into is arms. "If I know something so important, why don't they torture me for the information?"

"They did, Saxon. Where do you think all your scars really came from? You are no stunt man, any more than you are a football player or a construction worker."

• • •

Saxon is curled up naked into a ball on a bed. Several large burly men are gathered around him beating him with wooden rods. Saxon screams in pain while covering his head with his arms, trying to protect his skull.

• • •

Saxon goes rigid with the memory. Irina reaches up to turn his face toward hers. "And they tried every drug they had."

•　　•　　•

Saxon is strapped naked, except for the dozen wires attached all over, to a table with an IV hooked up to his arm. He appears delirious. Several shadowy figures hover about the table observing, adjusting the IV, noting monitors that track his condition.

•　　•　　•

Saxon begins to tremble in her arms, but Irina presses on. "They had to stop. They were afraid they would kill you, or destroy your brain. They'd never learn what they need to know if you died or turned into a vegetable. That's why your head is so foggy. They used some powerful drugs on you."

"Who are they?" Saxon snarls. "Who are you?"

Irina smiles. "They are the bad guys. We are the good guys."

"Of course." Saxon breaks from her embrace. "So what's the plan?"

"To get you away from them." Irina stands. "There's a car waiting for us in the forest." She helps Saxon to his feet. She puts an arm around his waist and leads him back toward the church.

Saxon stops abruptly. "You said the forest."

"They're watching us, Saxon. They'd never let us walk off into the trees. There's another way. Through the church."

Saxon backs away from the closed church door.

"I know you don't want to go back in there. I know all those human bones remind you of something horrible. But you must. It's the only way." Irina urges him up to the door. Opens it. She takes Saxon's hand. It is trembling. He is trembling, worse than before. She urges him forward, smiling. "You are so strong, Saxon. That is one thing for sure. You would have to be to stand up to their torture like you did."

Saxon scowls at her.

"And to stand up to this psychological torment. They're trying to trick you into revealing what you refused to give up under torture and drugs."

"I hope so. The alternative is much worse."

"What alternative?"

"That my mind snapped. Under the torture and drugs. That all this is some insane fantasy. My mind playing out its dying moments."

Irina reaches up to stroke his face with tenderness. "I'm no fantasy."

"But which side are you on?" Saxon turns away and walks on into the church.

Irina falls into step behind him. "I'm on your side." She follows him into the church. The room is empty.

Saxon glances back at Irina as the door closes. "Where is everybody?"

"The tour continues out the back. I told the guide we'd wait by the bus for them to

finish." Irina takes the lead, grabbing Saxon by the hand and towing him behind her.

He follows without protest, gazing all around. "So how are we getting out of the church?

Without them seeing us?"

"Through the catacombs." Irina leads him to a small door, which she opens.

Stairs lead down out of sight into a dank gloom. Saxon pulls back, but Irina smiles at him in encouragement. "You can handle this."

"How do you know what I can handle?"

"You seem to handle yourself very well. You've been well-trained."

"So I could really be a football player? Or a stunt man?"

"Or an Interpol agent."

•　　　•　　　•

In an office, Saxon, unscarred, clean-cut in a suit, sits at a table with several other suits and several lab coat types. They are deep in discussion.

•   •   •

Saxon freezes. "A what?"

Irina runs ahead, motioning for him to hurry. "The car should be here by now."

Saxon stumbles down the stairs after. At the foot of the stairs is the entrance to the catacombs. Beyond is a narrow dark rock tunnel lined with countless human skulls and bones. Irina is running ahead into the dark. But Saxon freezes at the entrance.

•   •   •

Saxon, back in his cage, in his undershorts, filthy and battered, watches as several armed guards stumble past him. They appear very sick. In the background a dozen or so bodies lie dead where they fell. For once, there is no music, no strident violin. All he hears are the screams of the dying. The Doctor crashes up to his cage. He appears as sick as the others. Blood oozes from his mouth, his nose, his ears, his eyes. With a scream of agony, he collapses.

•   •   •

Saxon grabs the wall to keep from falling, staring after Irina's retreating form.

"Wait!"

"We can't! Come on!" Irina disappears into the shadows.

With a supreme effort of will, Saxon pushes off from the wall and staggers after her. He glances to one side, to find piles of bones and skulls just inches from his face.

•   •   •

Watching the guards stumble and crawl about in their death throes, Saxon reaches through the bars to fish out the keys from the unmoving Doctor's pocket.

•　　　•　　　•

Saxon stumbles on, looking to his other side. More bones, more skulls, inches away, seeming to stare at him, to laugh at him, to reach out for him.

•　　　•　　　•

Saxon, now clad in ragged blood-stained military fatigues, walks among the dead bodies of the Doctor and the guards, and his comrades. He is the only person stirring. Everyone else is dead, lying in pools of blood, blood having issued from their mouths, noses, eyes, ears, blood having soaked through their pants, front and back.

•　　　•　　　•

Saxon stumbles on, turning away from all the bones, determined to stare straight ahead into the dark of the hallway as Irina's rapid footsteps echo away from him.

•　　　•　　　•

Saxon walks among the dead bodies, spraying them with automatic weapon fire. He empties the gun, drops it and stoops to pick up another from the grasp of a dead guard lying on the ground, then resumes walking and firing.

•　　　•　　　•

Gunfire echoes in Saxon's head as he crashes to the ground. He looks up. The neatly stacked skulls all glare down at him. Laugh at him. Bony fingers point down at him. "Death," the teeth clack. "You are death."

•　　　•　　　•

Saxon sits calmly before a bonfire of papers and computers. He thumbs through a stack of classical music CDs. One by one he takes them out of their jewel cases and snaps them in half. He tosses the broken disks into the blaze, above which hover several skulls. There is mirth in their empty eye sockets. The crackling fire utters one word. "Death."

•　　•　　•

Saxon rolls limp over onto his back. He casts his frantic gaze from side to side, at all of the human skulls and bones looming above him, gazing down on him, threatening to engulf him, to bury him. There is an avalanche as they fall.

•　　•　　•

Saxon sits contemplating a vial of pale liquid, holding it up, turning it this way and that as he studies it in the flickering light of the dying bonfire. Many other such vials are lined up in racks before him.

•　　•　　•

"IRINA!!"

"We have Irina."

Saxon looks wildly about. No bones are on him, none have fallen, they are all still arranged along the walls. What he sees is Philip standing over him smoking a cigarette. He spreads his arms wide. "Some place, isn't it?" He smashes his cigarette out on a skull.

"My squad was ambushed," Saxon babbles. "The survivors were used as guinea pigs. But I didn't die. The Doctor couldn't believe it. He had to find out why. But he got careless. He couldn't believe I was sick. He thought there was no way. I couldn't be sick, and still be alive. So he got careless. And paid the price. Same as all the others. All of them. They took their lead from the Doctor. He got careless. They all got careless. Everyone died. Except me."

Philip leaned down. "Why you, Saxon? What makes you special?"

Saxon flails about the floor. While Philip watches with little apparent interest, he clutches at bones and skulls to pull himself up. "Where'd you go? Yesterday? At the inn?"

Philip stares blank-faced, without replying.

Saxon scrambles up to his feet. He clutches at the shelves of bones for support. Still holding on with both hands, he looks beyond Philip into the dark tunnel Irina disappeared into. "Irina!"

"She's gone, Sax. We've got her."

Saxon jerks around, nearly falling. Obinna stands behind him. Saxon ignores him. "Irina!"

"You're making too much noise." Obinna punches him in the stomach, knocking the air out of him. Saxon doubles over.

Philip punches him in the kidney. Saxon falls to his knees. "Where is it, Saxon?"

Obinna punches him in the face. Saxon collapses on the floor. "Where'd you hide it, Saxon?" The two men kick his defenseless form, front and back.

Saxon doesn't even try to cover up as the two men dribble him like a football.

·   ·   ·

The book, "The Metamorphosis", by Franz Kafka, is on a shelf in a library, lined up alongside many others. A shaky hand reaches out for it, takes it down, opens it. The hand is Saxon's. He is naked, covered in scars and bruises and cuts, exhausted, totally spent. He collapses to the floor with the book. Begins to read.

·   ·   ·

A large bonfire blazes in the middle of the cave. Saxon, dressed in military fatigues, stands before it, watching computers, books, ledgers, graph papers, computer disks, folders, files, all forms of information burn. On the floor before him is a stereo boombox. He stomps it and stomps it, then kicks the splintered plastic and electronics into the fire.

•   •   •

A cockroach crawls across the floor of the library. A hand snatches it up. The hand is Saxon's. He raises the captured bug up before his face to study it. Sitting naked on the floor, he looks the same as before. Except he is strangely calm, studying the bug. He glances down to the book lying on the floor beside him. "The Metamorphosis". He picks up the book, opens the cover, places the bug inside, then quickly slams the book closed. He opens it back up, to stare at the just-smashed bug.

10

A TREMENDOUS EXPLOSION!! *Lights up the night! And illuminates Saxon, now wearing the bloody torn fatigues, standing a safe distance away in the gorge through which he had approached the cave, watching.*

• • •

Saxon's eyes flutter open, with the fading roar of the explosion echoing. His face is bruised and swollen and cut.

"My God, Sajon! What happened!?" Valeria's crying face looms up before him. "Who did this to you?"

Saxon looks beyond her. He is in a room at the inn. His room? Which one? Six? Twelve? Nine? He is stretched out on his back in bed. "Where's Irina?"

Valeria, who he now notices is wearing a nightgown the same shade of black as Irina's dress, rushes away into the bathroom. "Who?"

"Is she dead?"

Valeria hurries back with a damp washcloth and a towel. "I don't know who or what you are talking about! They said you got sick, that you got separated from the tour group. They left you behind. When they came back for you, they found you beaten up like this. We'll go to the embassy ..."

"...Which embassy? British? Columbian?"

"Columbian! Of course! And make a report ..."

"Stop lying!" Saxon sits up and shoves her away. "There is no Colombian embassy in Prague."

Valeria freezes, stricken.

Caught in a lie, Saxon wonders? Or perhaps she just didn't know. And how did he know this? He shakes his head in disgust. "It doesn't matter. I'll wake up tomorrow and you'll be gone." Saxon barks a laugh. "I'll wake up tomorrow and *I'll* be gone, and someone else will be in this body." He snorts. "Pity him."

Valeria steps up and tries once again to attend to his injuries. "Stop talking crazy, Sajon. You scare me."

Saxon shrugs off her hands and peers into her worried eyes. "That's funny. You scare the hell out of me." He moves surprisingly fast, grabbing both her wrists. "Who are you?"

Valeria lunges back in a panic, but she can't get away, her hands are caught in his grip. "Your wife of ten years."

·   ·   ·

In a sun-drenched simple kitchen Valeria and Saxon stand side by side at the sink washing and drying dishes. They seem happily content as they work.

·   ·   ·

Saxon releases one of her hands to smack his forehead, then whips his head back and forth. "That was a good one." He glares at her with dangerous eyes. "Whoever beamed that one into my head did a real good job."

Valeria sags down before him onto her knees, sobbing, her one wrist still clamped tight by him.

Saxon yanks her back up as he stands. "Can it? You're a terrible actress." He releases her wrist and flings her back onto the bed. "I'm no more married to you than I am a football player or a movie stunt man or a construction worker."

Valeria gazes up at him through her tears. "I didn't realize you were this sick. We need to go home right away."

"Tell me more about our happy home. I want to see what other warm and fuzzy domestic fantasies flash into my head."

Valeria snivels her tears dry. "Maybe I can get our tickets changed, for an earlier flight. We've got to get you back home."

Saxon dismisses her with a wave as he looks himself over. Someone has stripped him down to his undershorts. Valeria? Obinna? Philip?

"What are you doing?"

Saxon ignores her as he staggers up to the dresser and continues looking his wounds over in the mirror.

"We need to get you to a doctor."

•   •   •

The Doctor's vile visage hangs in the air directly above the table he is strapped to face-up in his undershorts.

•   •   •

Saxon shivers, shakes the haunting image off, then staggers on into the bathroom. "No need for a doctor. I'll take care of this myself. I've been well-trained. As something." Saxon peers into the mirror at his bruised puffy blood-caked face. Valeria's reflection appears in the open doorway behind him. "Worried I'll run off?"

"No. Just worried."

He turns to face her.

•   •   •

Valeria prances in the same black night gown before the bed Saxon is sprawled across. The open gift box it came in is on the dresser. She smiles, happy as she models the sexy satin. Saxon looks on with obvious yearning.

•   •   •

Saxon head butts her. "Stop it."
Valeria staggers back out of the bathroom.
He catches her to keep her from falling. "Don't do that again."
"Do what?"
Realizing she is steady on her feet, he releases her and smiles. "That was just a love tap. I can hit a lot harder."
"You have never hit me before."
"I don't know that." Saxon turns back to the mirror to tend to his face. "Don't worry. You'll be gone in the morning."
"Why do you keep saying that?"
"Just wait and see. You will be."

•   •   •

Saxon sits naked on the floor of the library, covered in scars and bruises, exhausted, spent. On the floor in front of him is the book, "The Metamorphosis". Across the room is the sofa he is staring at. Some large dark form moves beneath it, something pokes out from underneath. A giant insect is under the sofa. It is too large to be completely concealed by the sofa, part of it sticks out. Saxon contemplates the giant insect.

•   •   •

The room in the inn is dimly lit by early morning sunlight seeping in around the closed wooden shutters. Two forms sleep beneath the covers. Valeria awakens, in the same black nightgown as before. She sits up and stretches. She smiles as she pulls the covers down. Saxon lies unmoving beside her.

Saxon's eyes snap open. He smiles. A half-dozen cockroaches crawl out of his mouth. Valeria SCREAMS!

•   •   •

Saxon opens his eyes with a start, still hearing Valeria's scream. He quickly touches his mouth, his face, his pillow, the sheets, searching for the insects he had been dreaming about. He finds none. He feels his face, winces. The new injuries are still there and hurt like real. No theatrical make-up this time.

Saxon turns to look at the person twisted up beneath the covers next to him. It is female, but her back is turned and Saxon can't tell much about her. Her hair, the same shade as Valeria's, is a tangle. A strap of a black nightgown is looped over her upturned shoulder. Saxon turns back the sheet and leans over to look. It is Valeria. She has a small lump in the middle of her forehead from the head-butt. She opens her eyes and looks sleepily up at him. "I'm still here."

"I see that. Change of tactics." Saxon throws back the sheet and climbs out of bed. Valeria watches with concern as he stumbles around the bed to the wooden shutters. He throws them open and steps out onto the balcony, shielding his eyes as he looks out over the cobblestone plaza. The sun is well up. People are seated around the tables before the café drinking coffee. He has slept late.

Valeria steps up behind him. "You seem calmer this morning."

"Maybe I'm coming to accept that I am totally screwed up. That I will never learn who I really am."

Valeria hugs Saxon from behind and lays her head on his shoulder. "You just need time to heal. You hit your head on concrete steps at the stadium. That was some lick you took. It could have killed you."

•   •   •

Saxon lies flat on his back on the steps of an upper level of the stadium. Huddled around and staring down at him with grave concern are Philip, Obinna, and Bozidar.

•   •   •

Saxon smiles at her. "Maybe it did."

"What are you talking about?"

Saxon shakes his head. "What's to keep me from just walking away?"

Valeria tightens her hold on him from behind. "Where would you go?"

"Exactly. Where would I go? I know of no other place than this. It wouldn't matter anyway, would it? You'd follow me. They'd find me. No matter where I went." Saxon spins and grabs her neck with both hands. "What do you want from me?" Valeria is terror-stricken. She's not acting, Saxon assesses. The fear in her face looks real. She knows he is capable of killing her. Valeria tries to get away, but Saxon has a firm grip on her throat as he forces her back off the balcony into the room. "I never hit you? In ten years of marriage? That's hard to believe. I'm a violent person, and you lie through your teeth."

Valeria struggles to get free.

Saxon tightens his grip. "Philip and Ben think I hid something, think I know where something is. What?"

Valeria, in a panic, fights to get free. Her ineffectual fists beat at his face.

Saxon laughs as he throttles her. "You'll have to do better than that. I've been beaten too many times for it to bother me anymore." Saxon squeezes harder. "Tell me what's going on, wife, and I'll let you live."

Valeria pulls on his hands with all her might, but she can't budge them. Her red face begins to turn purple.

Saxon squeezes harder.

•   •   •

Saxon, clean and uninjured and wearing clean military fatigues, has his hands locked around a man's throat, while the man, similarly dressed, fights to get free. They are locked in mortal hand-to-hand combat, and Saxon is winning. Until a whistle blows. Saxon at once releases the man. They smile at each other, the man rubbing his throat. Saxon looks up. They are in a gym, with a dozen other men.

•　　　•　　　•

Stunned, Saxon releases Valeria. She collapses, gasping for air, to the floor at his feet. He doesn't notice. "I've been trained to fight. I'm a soldier. An agent. Special forces. Of some kind." Stepping over her still-gasping body writhing on the floor, he paces. "I was on a mission. Was captured. Used for experiments. Then beaten and tortured. They think I know something. What?" He drops down to the floor and grabs Valeria's hair, wrenching her head up to peer into her terrified face. "What? What are they after?" Seeing no knowledge, merely terror in her eyes, Saxon throws her head back down and rises. "I'll find out myself."

Saxon goes to the wardrobe and yanks out pants and shirt. Behind him Valeria crawls across the floor, pulls herself up onto a bed and collapses, never taking her eyes off him. With his hands full of clothes, Saxon stops to look at the nightstand. The book, "The Metamorphosis", is there. Saxon lunges over to it. When Valeria scrambles across the bed away from him, fearful he is coming after her again, he dismisses her with a snort and snatches up the book. He opens the cover. The smashed bug is there.

•　　　•　　　•

Saxon pops a cockroach into his mouth, chews it, swallows it.

•　　　•　　　•

Saxon puts a cockroach inside a book, quickly slams the cover shut on it. It is "The Metamorphosis". He opens the cover. Inside, the freshly-smashed bug.

•   •   •

SLAM!

Saxon looks up to see Valeria gone, the just-slammed door still reverberating. He sets the book aside and begins dressing.

11

S AXON, CARRYING "THE METAMORPHOSIS", walks down the stairs into the lobby. The desk clerk glances up at him. Saxon smiles, waves. "If you see my wife running around in her nightgown, tell her it's safe to go back to the room and get dressed now. I'm going for a walk." The desk clerk stares without replying at Saxon as he crosses the room. Saxon looks to the tour desk, but the tour operator is not there. He strides with a sure step out the door.

Saxon walks outside and passes by the cafe. The violin player is performing. Tchaikovsky's Violin Concerto. Saxon scowls. He has heard this before.

●　　　●　　　●

Saxon, beaten and bloody, in only undershorts, sits huddled in a small steel cage, while this same music plays.

•   •   •

The waiter watches him with a grim expression. Saxon waves, grimace in place, then dismisses the music and walks on into the street. The violin player stops playing as Saxon walks away, following his progress until he is gone. He then puts his violin away in its instrument case.

Saxon strolls, looking all about like any tourist. But other people stare at him with worry, alarmed by his beaten-up face. Turning a corner, he comes to a puppet shop. He looks over the many puppets displayed in the window. He spies the one he had watched two days ago, at the cafe.

•   •   •

The puppet maker yanks the strings, making the puppet jerk in spasms across his table toward Saxon like it is attacking.

•   •   •

"Keep looking over my puppets as we talk."

Saxon's eyes dart to find the puppet maker standing in his open doorway. They dart back to the shop window. "Why should we talk?"

"So I can tell you about Irina."

Saxon jerks around in surprise to stare at the puppet maker.

He sighs, shaking his head, and whispers, "Some spy you are." He calls out in a loud voice, "Come inside. I have many more to show you." He turns back into his shop, and Saxon follows. The puppet maker goes behind his counter and takes out a puppet, which he holds up to pretend to show Saxon. "We got Irina away from them at Sedlec."

Saxon walks up to the counter and pretends to be interested in the puppet he is being shown. "She's safe?"

"Yes. You can see for yourself."

"How?"

"Go to the Charles Bridge. Find the statue of John of Nepomuk. It's the only bronze statue there." He smiles. "Rub it for luck. It looks like you need all you can get. Someone will meet you there and take you to Irina."

"Then what?"

"Irina has a car. And she has papers for you. She'll drive you to the airport."

"They'll let me fly out?"

"They own the inn you are staying at. They don't own the whole country. They can't stop us in public."

"That didn't bother them at Kutna Hora."

"They knew the tour was going there. They were ready. Now they don't know what we have planned."

Saxon hears someone enter behind him. He looks to see it is the violin player, carrying his instrument case.

"Take a closer look at the workmanship of this one."Saxon turns back around to see the puppet maker holding up a different puppet.

Ignoring the puppet, Saxon leans in to whisper. "This man followed me from the inn."

The puppet maker presses on. "Look closely at the detail of the face."

Saxon peers at the puppet maker in confusion, then does as requested, focusing on the puppet's face.

•　　•　　•

The Doctor's demonic face approaches Saxon strapped to the medical examining table in his undershorts. The Doctor holds a hypodermic filled with the same colored solution that had been in the vial Saxon had held and examined. While Tchaikovsky's Violin Concerto plays.

•　　•　　•

Saxon looks up in surprise, locking onto the puppet maker's face.

He jerks upright, reaching for the back of his neck as he spins around. The violin player, his empty instrument case open at his feet, holds a gun. Saxon pulls a dart from his neck, sees what it is, then tosses it down and dashes for the door. He takes two steps, crashes to the floor. He struggles to get up, but fails and collapses flat onto his back. As he looks up, the puppet maker and the violin player loom into his line of vision.

"Not just the puppet, Saxon." The puppet maker drops down low. "Look closely at the details of *my* face."

Saxon forces his waning awareness to concentrate on the puppet maker's near face.

•　　•　　•

The Doctor's demonic face once again looms above him, filling his vision.

•　　•　　•

"You're dead. I watched you die."

"You remember seeing me die. But you remember many things. Too many things. They all can't be real. Which memories are real, Saxon? Which are fantasies?"

The puppet maker sweeps a gentle hand across Saxon's eyes. When he removes his hand, Saxon's eyes are closed.

12

*S*AXON, NAKED AND BADLY-BEATEN, *sits on the bare wooden floor of the library. Next to him on the floor is the book, "The Metamorphosis". Several feet away is a couch. Below it, sticking out from under part-way, is a giant insect. Saxon stares at it. "Are you real?"*

"Yes."

"What are you?"

"Death."

Dead naked male bodies piled tightly together, much like the tombstones in the Old Jewish Cemetery in Prague, their faces locked in rictal agony and covered in dried blood that had streamed from their mouths, ears, eyes, noses. Elsewhere, dried blood all around their groins and their buttocks, from where it had issued from those orifices. Saxon sits on the ground leaning back against a blood-soaked body.

Looking around, he sees he is now in the Old Jewish Cemetery. He spies the giant insect, mostly hidden beneath several other blood-soaked bodies, as it had been mostly hidden beneath the couch in the library. Saxon picks up a bare skull, like one of the many he had seen at Sedlec, looks it over, then tosses it aside. "Why haven't you killed me? Like all the others?"

"YOU killed ME." One of the insect's many legs reaches out from underneath the bloody pile of flesh, pointing. Saxon looks. It is pointing at "The Metamorphosis" lying on a grave next to him. Saxon picks it up, opens the cover. The smashed bug is there. "You smashed me."

Saxon sits naked on the wooden floor of the library once again, an open book in his lap. He puts a cockroach inside the book, quickly slaps the cover shut on it. The cover is seen to be that of "The Metamorphosis". He opens the cover. Inside is the gooey remains of the just-smashed bug. "Why?"

"Why do people press things into books?" Saxon looks up to the giant bug beneath the couch once again. "To preserve them, so they will be remembered."

"Why would I want to remember a bug?"

"Because of what I represent. But you also ate me."

Saxon snatches up a cockroach scurrying across the floor. He holds it up before his face to study its wriggling form. Then pops it into his mouth, chews it, swallows it. He looks back to the giant insect beneath the couch. "Why?"

"You ate death to live."

"Was I starving?"

"No. You ate death to become death."

"That makes no sense."

"You are the living death."

•   •   •

Saxon opens his eyes.

"Daddy's awake!"

Saxon jerks upright. A six-year-old girl stands smiling beside the bed. She runs to the closed door and opens it. "Daddy woke up!"

Saxon rubs his face hard, trying to force awareness. He scans his surroundings.

This does not look like any of the rooms he has seen at the inn in Prague. He is in a more modern style of bed. The entire room, a small and simple bedroom, is more modern. Displayed on a dresser is a photo of him, the little girl, and an attractive young woman, all smiling. In the photo Saxon wears a familiar football jersey.

The little girl returns, accompanied by the woman in the photo. She and the girl approach the side of the bed. "How are you feeling, darling?" the woman asks.

Saxon studies one face, then the other. "Where am I?"

"You're home."

"And where is home?"

"Our house. Outside of Helsinki."

Saxon smiles. "I wondered what language I was speaking. Finnish?"

"Of course, Daddy. Don't be silly."

Saxon smiles at the girl. He reaches out to stroke her hair. She is perfectly at ease with this, but he notices the woman flinch. He drops his hand. "How did I get home?"

"I brought you." A heavily-accented female voice answers in English.

Saxon looks beyond the pair at his bedside to see Irina walk into the room. His smile flees his face as he replies in English. "How?"

"Calm down and try to remember. I know your mind is a mess. But try."

Saxon lies back and closes his eyes.

•   •   •

Saxon walks the streets of Old Town in Prague. Up ahead is the Charles Bridge.

Saxon stands on the bridge next to the statue of John of Nepomuk, staring down into the river. The woman from the tour desk at the inn joins him.

Saxon and the tour operator walk down a deserted alley like the one he and Shino had strolled. They turn a corner, and there stands Irina.

The tour operator drives a car, with Saxon and Irina in the back. Irina hands him identification documents and he flips through them. He sees they are Finnish.

The car approaches an airport.

• • •

Saxon opens his eyes, staring up at the three expectant female faces. He produces a grim approximation of a smile. "These memories are like clockwork. Push a button, out pops a memory."

Irina tries to reassure him. "We got you out, Saxon. You're home now, with your family."

Saxon shakes his head, looking from one face to the next. The woman sits on the edge of the bed and leans toward him. Saxon scoots away from her. "Don't pretend to be my wife," he warns in Finish. "I nearly choked to death the last woman who tried that."

Irina places a hand on the woman's shoulder. "Katri, I told you it wouldn't be easy. You promised to help, not hinder."

Saxon looks to Irina, speaking in English. "Katri is her name?" He looks to the girl and inquires in Finish. "So what is the name of my darling daughter?"

"Marja, daddy." She flings herself on him to give a hug. "Don't be silly."

Saxon returns the hug.

• • •

Saxon plays with Marja, rolling across the grass with her. She laughs with delight in his arms.

• • •

Saxon looks to see Katri's pensive expression. "So she really is your daughter?" He releases the hug. "Don't worry. I would never harm a child."

Katri pulls Marja off the bed. "Let daddy be, Marja. He needs to rest." She leads her out of the room.

Saxon watches the door close behind them. He reverts to English. "That is a cruel riposte, using a child. You people are truly sadistic."

"You've been in sadistic hands, Saxon. But that's over. We're going to help you recover."

"We? They? Who are they? Who are we?" Saxon looks to the nightstand. 'The Metamorphosis' is there. "I see my book is here."

"You insisted we bring it."

"So you packed it for me. How considerate." His roving eyes lock onto the family photo. "I play football after all?"

"HIFK Fotboll, when you get the chance. You are quite good."

Saxon's eyes settle on a calendar. "How many days has it been?"

"We flew you out yesterday."

Saxon closes his eyes. Opens them seconds later. "Why no memories of the flight? Of my arrival home last night?"

"Your brain is working erratically …"

"… but not too erratically, I hope. There is something in there you need to get out." Saxon throws back the sheet and jumps up out of bed. His legs fold beneath him and he hits the floor hard.

Irina runs around the bed to help him. "Saxon. Be careful. You've been hurt enough."

Saxon shrugs her off and fights his way back up to sit on the edge of the bed. "How's my Finnish? Is it passable? Does this mean I was born and raised in Finland?" He closes his eyes then opens them again, like before. "Why no memories of my happy Scandinavian childhood?" He looks himself over. Clad in only undershorts, he sees his upper body is covered in bruises. "The beating Ben and Phil gave me is still fresh, so I guess it's not been too many days. I see I'm wearing different underwear." He smiles up at Irina. "I guess I should thank you for that, putting clean underwear on me. Did you give me a bath, too?"

"I've tried to take care of you, Saxon."

"Valeria tried to take care of me, too. Aren't you afraid I'll wring your neck, like I did her?"

Irina smiled. "Should I be worried?"

"No. I would never kill you. You are the only person in the whole world who might possibly be telling me the truth." Irina leans over to kiss him, but he leans away. "I'm a married man, Irina. You shouldn't be kissing me. One of my wives might get jealous."

Irina leans away, smiling. "Rest. Try to relax. It really is over. Their drugs will work their way out of your system. You'll start thinking clearly in a day or two. Then no one will have to tell you the answers. You'll know them."

"And the truth shall set me free? What if there is no truth. Only messed-up people."

"That wouldn't be a world worth fighting for. And you are a fighter, Saxon." Irina turns to go.

"You said before I'm an Interpol agent. Am I still one today?"

"Yes. Now try to rest. We'll talk more later." Irina walks out and closes the door.

Saxon remains seated on the edge of the bed staring at the closed door for a long moment. Then, carefully, slowly, he rises to his feet. Holding onto whatever is at hand, he slowly, shakily, makes his way over to the curtained window. He pulls the curtain back to look out. He sees a small backyard. The shrubbery, the trees — by the flora this could be Finland. Also, a swing set and sandbox, and toys scattered all about. All bordered by a tall privacy fence.

Saxon is about to let the curtain close when something catches his eye. He peers at something in the back corner of the yard. A large mushroom.

•   •   •

In the trees near the road peasants are bent over gathering something from the ground. "What are they doing?"

"Picking mushrooms," Irina answers. "Czech forests are filled with large ones. Every fall the peasants harvest them."

•   •   •

Saxon leans heavily on the window sill gazing out into the backyard at the single large mushroom. "So much for the only person in the whole world who might possibly be telling me the truth." He makes his way back to the bed with care. Stretching out, he picks up the book. He opens the cover and stares at the smashed bug. "I am the living death."

•   •   •

Saxon sits naked on the bare wooden floor of the library holding 'The Metamorphosis'. Across the room is the sofa with the giant insect beneath it sticking part way out. "What is real?"

"Look inside."

Saxon opens the cover. The smashed bug is there. "You are inside."

"Inside the book and inside you."

Saxon looks up from the book. "You are death. So only death is real?"

"And death is inside you. So you are real. The living death is real."

"The living death. What does that mean?"

"It is what you have become. You pressed a bug into a book about a bug, so you would remember. And you have eaten a bug. You have metamorphosed, Saxon, like Gregor Samsa. Metamorphosed into a giant bug. A terrible weapon."

•   •   •

Saxon sits up, in bed with the open book lying in his lap. He has fallen asleep while reading. The door opens, rousing Saxon. He looks to see Irina enter.

Irina is followed by two men in suits carrying briefcases. "I'm sorry, Saxon. The American DEA agents say this can't wait any longer."

Saxon struggles to compose himself. He sits up straighter and lays his book aside. "Fascinating book. Stirs up the most vivid memories."

Irina and the two men freeze for a moment, looking at him. Then the two men brush past Irina and open their briefcases on the bed.

"Do I get to learn now who I really am?"

"You really are Saxon Hedges," Irina answers.

"That's just a name. Which life goes with it?"

"That of an Interpol agent."

"An improvement over construction worker." He glances at the photo on the dresser. "Though I rather like the idea of being a football player."

One of the American DEA agents barks. "No more joking around. You've got to tell us what you know."

Saxon looks beyond him to Irina. "He's not doing it right. He's supposed to ask me what's the last thing I remember."

The other American DEA agent snaps open a map and spreads it out on the bed. "Sax! Knock it off! We need to know where you hid it!"

Still ignoring the two Americans, he looks to Irina again. "Do I know them?"

"You've worked with them for the last six months."

"Yeah?" He looks to the one who had spoken to him. "Then what's my pet name for my wife?"

"Vallie."

"Ha. That was yesterday's wife. No stuffed animal for you."

"Saxon," Irina says, "please settle down."

"How can he claim to be a good DEA Agent if he can't even keep the names of my fake wives straight?" He looks back to the DEA agent. "Today I'm married to Katri, buddy."

The two agents look to Irina. She sighs then looks out the door. Valeria walks in. "This is your wife, Saxon. The woman you've been married to for ten years."

Saxon looks to the dresser. The framed family photo is gone. He looks back to Valeria. "Is that so? So where's our darling daughter? Marja, is it? My God, I would never agree to a name like that."

Valeria appears as distraught as before. "We don't have a daughter."

"No?" Saxon clambers out of bed, knocking the briefcases out of his way as he goes.

"Grab him," Irina calls out. "He's going to fall." The two DEA Agents start towards him.

Saxon is unsteady on his feet, but waves them off. "No. I'll be careful. I won't fall. This time." He limps over to the window and pulls the curtain back. He gazes out at the same back yard as before, only there is no swing set, no sandbox, no toys. But the mushroom is still there. "You got all of her toys out. But you left the mushroom." There is silence behind him. He spins back around, to catch the four of them shooting hooded looks at each other. "This isn't Finland. We're still in the Czech Republic." They all four stare in return without replying. He hobbles about the room, attempting to pace, but keeps losing his balance and banging into things, nearly falling but catching himself at the last moment. "Did you really overlook the mushroom? Or did you leave it there on purpose? Did you intend for me to see it? So I'd think I was still in the Czech Republic? While I'm actually in Finland? Or Columbia, since I'm married to Vallie again? Where are we? Columbia? Finland? The Czech Republic?"

Irina walks over to intercept Saxon's erratic pacing, grabbing him by the arms. "Saxon. Settle down."

Saxon gazes deep into her eyes. "Whose side? Whose side are you on?"

"Your side."

"Yes, but which side is that?"

"Why don't you just tell us about your dreams."

"My dreams? Ahh, yes, my dreams. What's the last thing I remember? My dreams, of course. I just woke up from them." Saxon shrugs Irina off. "I'm not giving you my dreams." He staggers over to the bed and collapses once again. Looks down at the open map. It shows eastern Afghanistan and western Pakistan. "The 'Stans, yes." With an excellent Oliver Hardy accent, "Stan, here is another nice mess you've gotten me into." He drops the accent. "Funny, I've been dreaming about deserts and caves and … and …" He looks from one expectant face to another. "But I'm sure you know that already. You put the dreams there."

"No, Saxon," Irina says. "The dreams are real."

"My dreams are real and my waking life a fiction. If that's not fucked up then what is?"

The American DEA agent who had spoken before jerks his head at Valeria. "Get her out of here. We need to get down to business."

Irina leads Valeria out of the room.

The other American DEA agent focuses on Saxon. "We have to know where you hid the drugs."

Saxon looks back and forth from one agent to the other.

"You were tracking a potent new kind of opium. Derived from a new bio-engineered poppy plant. Heroin ten times as addictive as anything else on the market."

"It could literally rip Western civilization apart."

"You were on the trail of the biologist who crafted this new drug."

"Tracking him back to the opium fields in Afghanistan where the new poppy was growing."

"You assassinated the biologist and destroyed his formula and took the only sample of this new opium that exists."

"But you knew you were being pursued. So you hid it. Somewhere in here." He waves a hand across the open map. "But then they caught you. They tortured you, nearly drove you insane with their drugs, trying to force the hiding place from you."

"But you were so tough, Sax. You ARE so tough. You didn't give it up."

"By the time we got you away from them you were a wreck. Your head was so messed up from their drugs you wouldn't tell us, either. Where you hid it."

"We wanted to wait until you were well. But we can't. They are scouring the countryside looking for it."

"We can't let them find it. We've got to beat them to it. Or all your suffering will be for nothing."

"So you have to tell us. Right now, Saxon. Where did you hide it?" The two agents look from Saxon's face to the map open before him.

Saxon barks a laugh. "Nothing, guys. Sorry. No flashes of insight, no sudden memories popping into my head. You're losing your touch. It's not working this time." He stops laughing and snatches the map off the bed, wadding it up before their faces. "This is the lamest fiction yet. Everybody knows the poppy fields are in western Afghanistan, not eastern." Saxon throws the balled map down onto the floor. "But you showed me a map of eastern Afghanistan and western Pakistan. So I know where something important is hidden there. What is it you are really looking for, guys?"

The two agents look to Irina, who had quietly re-entered the bedroom. She steps forward. "Do you still trust me? A little?"

"No. I don't even trust myself. How can I? I'm a perfect stranger to myself. And my mother told me to never trust a stranger."

"You're not a perfect stranger to me."

"Then, please, introduce me to myself."

Irina nods. She turns to the two Americans. "You can go."

"Are you sure?" one of them asks.

"No. But nothing else has worked. It's time to try something different."

"Like the truth?" Saxon asks.

"Yes, Saxon, the truth."

Saxon staggers over to the closet to select some clothes. "I can't wait to hear the latest version of it." Saxon begins yanking clothes on. The two DEA Agents walk out. Leaving only Irina watching him struggle into jeans and a long sleeve cotton shirt. "These clothes are a good fit. Like always." Saxon sits on the edge of the bed to put on socks and shoes, then stands and walks across to the open door. He nods to Irina, and she walks out. He follows.

13

IRINA LEADS SAXON down a narrow hall into a living room. Seated are the puppet maker, the violin player, Valeria, and Katri with Marja in her lap. The two Americans stand by the front door. Saxon scans the faces. "So there *is* only one side."

The violin player takes out his instrument and begins playing the third movement of Sibelius Violin Concerto in D. The puppet maker takes up his puppet and makes it dance to the frantic pace of the music.

Saxon walks up to the puppet maker, bending down to gaze closely into his face. Saxon appears puzzled. "Now you don't look so much like him."

"There is some resemblance. But it was mostly the power of suggestion. That, and your brain addled by all the drugs."

Saxon acknowledges this with a grim smile. He walks over to Valeria. The bruises on her throat have darkened toward the violet end of the spectrum. She leans away from him in fear. The two Americans edge forward, ready to spring to her defense. But Irina motions for them to stay back.

Saxon raises his gaze to Valerias' face. "Sorry about the bruises on your throat. And the lump on your forehead. But you should be more careful who you marry. Hope there are no hard feelings." Saxon bends to kiss Valeria. She nervously returns his kiss.

He straightens and approaches Katri. "And a kiss for wife number two." He bends to kiss her. Katri, also, nervously returns his kiss. Saxon raises and contemplates Marja. Katri tightens her hold on her daughter, while Marja peers up at him from her mother's lap with a cloudy face, on the verge of tears. Saxon smiles. Speaking in Finnish, "I'm not angry with you for tricking me, Marja. You are a beautiful child. I'd be proud to have you for a daughter." The child breaks into a wide grin.

Saxon turns away to face Irina. "Now what?"

"Now it's time for you to meet the boss."

Saxon nods with approval and follows her out the front door, the Sebelius violin music still playing. They emerge from out of a small country cottage into a small front yard. In the driveway sits the car which in his memories had driven him to the airport. Behind the wheel sits the female tour operator. He glances back at the two Americans following them out of the house. "Bodyguards?"

Irina shrugs. "They've got their own car." Irina leads Saxon to the car waiting in the driveway. He glares after the two Americans as they walk toward the garage. "I wouldn't antagonize them any further, Saxon. You just kissed their wives."

"You mean one of those goons fathered that delightful little girl? The wonders of nature." Saxon climbs in back next to Irina and shuts the door. The tour operator starts the car and pulls out of the driveway onto a narrow country lane. Saxon glances out the rear window to see the two Americans follow in their car. He then leans forward. "Hello. Have any interesting places to take us to today? Your last tour was fascinating."

"No tour today," Irina says. "We're going back to the inn."

"I knew we were still in the Czech Republic. As well as I can know anything." Saxon leans back and focuses on Irina. "I was actually worried about you. That you had been captured."

"I appreciate your concern. Now, I'm sure you have plenty of questions."

"Actually, only one. I remember us making love. Was that real?"

Irina laughs. "No. That memory was to form an attachment between us. Most men feel protective of the women they've been intimate with."

"Then let's make it real." Saxon embraces Irina and kisses her.

Irina is surprised, and resists. The car pulls over and the female tour operator turns around with a gun aimed at Saxon's head. Breaking free of Saxon's embrace, Irina waves it away. "Go on. Slowly."

Saxon once again engages her mouth with his. This time Irina returns the passion. They stretch out across the rear seat and pull at each others' clothes. The tour operator smiles as she turns back around, setting the gun down on the seat next to her. She pulls back out onto the road.

A phone rings. The tour operator answers it. "What's going on?" one of the Americans driving behind them asks.

"Nothing," she replies. "Keep going. Just hang back." She ends the call then angles the rearview mirror so she can see down into the back seat. Saxon and Irina are now half-undressed and inventively entwined.

A little later the tour operator pulls the car up before the inn. The back car doors open. Irina emerges, tugging and arranging her clothes. Saxon emerges from the other side, not bothering with his disarrayed clothes. The trailing car pulls up and parks behind them. The two Americans remain in it, watching, as does the tour operator from behind the wheel of the car she is driving. Irina leads Saxon toward the inn. As they pass the courtyard cafe Saxon smiles and waves at the waiter. Saxon then follows Irina inside.

Irina walks across the lobby to a first floor hallway. As Saxon follows he glances to the front desk. The desk clerk watches closely, with his right hand out of sight below the counter. Saxon holds up both hands to show he is unarmed as he follows Irina down the first floor hall.

Irina leads Saxon to the closed door of room number one. She opens the unlocked door without knocking and enters. Saxon walks in behind her. This room is actually a suite. Standing just inside the door are two of the three young toughs who had ambushed Saxon and Shino by the river. One closes and locks the door, while the other holds a gun on Saxon. Saxon smiles at this, then continues into the room. Seated around the room are Philip, Obinna, Hanako, and the other young tough with his wrist in a sling. Saxon smiles upon seeing him. "If I'd known that fight was staged, I wouldn't have been so rough on you. Glad I didn't know."

Saxon smiles at Hanako. "You and Shino are not anybody's wives, I hope?"

Hanako shakes her head no without returning the smile.

Saxon scans the room. "By the way, where is Shino?"

"I don't know," Hanako replies. "Probably wandering around Old Town somewhere. She loves this place."

Saxon smiles, nodding at this. He glances to Philip. He sits balled up in a chair, appearing miserable. "What's the matter, Philip? You don't look well."

Philip returns a malevolent glare.

"He's coming down with something," Obinna answers for him. "I don't feel that hot myself. Some bug is going around."

Saxon guffaws. "Yes it is."

Irina stares at him with a curious eye. "Your spirits have certainly improved."

Saxon turns to Irina, standing right beside him. "Of course. I finally get to meet the brains behind all this." He gazes all about the room. "So? Where is he?"

Irina walks across the room to a large lavish chair at the front. She sits, beaming up at him. "Have a seat, Saxon. We have a lot to talk over."

As realization dawns, Saxon smiles in return. One of the young toughs steps up behind Saxon with a straight back chair. Saxon sits. This places him in the middle of the room, ringed by all the others. He looks to Irina. "Let's trade. You tell me something, I'll tell you something."

Irina nods in agreement.

"Why all the games? With my memory?"

"Ever try to recover files from a ruined hard drive?"

"I don't know if I ever have or not."

"That's what we've been trying to do with you. Once we gave up on extracting information from you in the usual ways, your mind was nearly ruined. But even a ruined hard drive retains information. So we tried to recover data from you in a different way. You needed a new operating system. So several different histories were layered into your consciousness, one on top of the other."

Saxon is intrigued. "That can be done?"

"You'd be amazed at how easily false memories can be planted in people. That's why a good police interrogator needs to guard against false confessions. He pounds away at his subjects so relentlessly he can actually convince some innocent ones that they committed a crime they didn't do."

"To what purpose? For me?"

"We thought if we overwhelmed you with a lot of conflicting false memories, your true memories would come to seem false, also. You'd be a lot more likely to tell us what we wanted to know if you couldn't distinguish your real memories from the false ones we had planted, between which were worth fighting to protect and which weren't." Irina falls silent as she gives Saxon a chance to mull over what he has just heard. Then she speaks again. "Now it's my turn."

Saxon nods his consent.

"Who are you?"

Saxon smiles. "Funny. That was going to be *my* next question. Who am I?"

"Whoever you are, you are very good. You survived the ambush in the desert, escaped from a sizeable force of fierce warriors, who you single-handedly wiped out, destroyed the cave complex, and withstood intense physical and psychological torture."

"I'm impressed with myself."

"When we caught you after you blew up the cave you had no identification on you. Are you Interpol? CIA? Special Forces? A mercenary?"

"I could be KGB. Are they still around?"

"No, you are not Russian."

Saxon replies in Russian. "Are you sure?"

Irina is perturbed, and so flustered she continues in Russian. "I would know if you were Russian."

"Would you?"

A loud groan comes from Philip. Everyone turns to look. He is doubled up in his chair, muscles spasming all over his knotted body. Saxon glances to Obinna. He is drenched in sweat.

Saxon reverts to English. "We're being rude, Irina. We should speak English so everyone else can keep up."

Irina reverts to English. "How many languages do you know?" After Saxon shrugs, she continues. "While you were delirious you sounded like the U.N. General Assembly, ranting in English, Russian, Czech, Spanish, Finnish, some others I didn't recognize."

"So you used those languages to invent your fantasies about my life."

"And that Kafka book. 'The Metamorphosis'. Why did you take that? We kept you locked up in the library of a house out in the country while we interrogated you. You found that book there and wouldn't let go of it. It had some significance for you. So when we brought you to Prague we brought the book along. Philip gave it back to you that first day at the inn."

•　　•　　•

Philip tosses a book across the room at the inn to Saxon, who catches it with his left hand.

•　　•　　•

Hearing a crash, Saxon turns to see Philip has fallen out of his chair onto the floor. Hanako goes to him. She lifts his face up. He appears to be in intense pain.

Irina turns to Hanako. "Does he need to go to the hospital?"

Hanako shrugs cluelessly. She wipes the heavy sweat from his brow, trying to ease him. Obinna looks on with growing concern, appearing worse himself by the minute.

"I needed the book to remind myself."

Saxon draws Irina's attention back to him. "Of what?"

"I realized my mind was in danger of snapping. So I left a secret note to myself. In a sort of code no one else would understand. To help me remember later."

"We went all through that book. Sentence by sentence. There was nothing. Except for that bug you killed."

Saxon smiles. "A smashed bug. Inside a book about a bug. Gregor and I have had some interesting conversations."

Hanako screams! Everyone turns to look. Philip groans, writhing in agony on the floor as blood flows from his mouth, nose, ears, eyes. Obinna jumps to his feet, pulling out his gun. With his other hand he holds his stomach, which is cramping so much he can't stand up straight. His gun weaves all around the room as he tries to aim for Saxon. "It's the virus! He's infected!"

Irina's calm is beginning to waver. "Impossible. He'd be dead."

"The Doctor thought that, too," Saxon says.

The two young toughs standing by the door draw their guns and approach Saxon from behind. Saxon turns to the advancing pair with a pleasant smile. "The last thing you want to do is kill me."

Obinna's gun waves all across the room as he grows unsteadier by the second. He glances at Irina as if asking permission to shoot Saxon.

Irina forestalls Obinna, then turns to Saxon. "And why is that?"

"I didn't hide the virus anywhere. I destroyed it. All of it. And I destroyed all of the Doctor's files. I burned them then blew the cave up."

"Then there is no reason to keep you alive any longer." Irina nods to the two young toughs.

Feeling two barrels press against the back of his skull, Saxon smiles. "Aren't you curious how I did it?"

Irina holds up a restraining hand. The two lower their guns and back away. She nods at Saxon to continue.

"Ever hear of Typhoid Mary?" Saxon looks around, but everyone merely stares back. He shrugs then continues. "I'm guessing the reason I was chosen to lead the search for your Doctor was that my genome showed me to carry a resistance to the virus we, whoever we is, knew he was working with. So I lived, to infect others. In the tight confines of the cave complex, the virus spread quickly. After they all succumbed to it, I shot their corpses up. Finding their bodies full of bullets, I knew you would look no further for the real cause of their deaths." Saxon turns back toward Obinna, who appears ready to collapse. He looks down at Philip in a rigid bloody ball on the floor. The front and back of his pants are now soaked with blood. Hanako scoots away from him, staring at him with revulsion. "So all that remains of the most terrible biological weapon ever developed is what the Doctor injected into me." Saxon smiles, tapping his chest with a finger. "Here. Inside me. Kill me and you lose this weapon forever."

"He's right!" Irina yells. "Don't kill him!"

Obinna collapses onto the floor, dropping his gun. Saxon nimbly snatches up the gun, backing away across the room. The two young toughs back away toward the door, their guns wavering uncertainly.

"DON'T SHOOT HIM!!" Irina screams.

The two glance indecisively at Irina, at Saxon, at each other, as they back all the way to the door. Saxon fires twice, drops each with a clean head shot. The third tough clumsily pulls at his gun with his uninjured hand. Irina fires a gun, killing him. Saxon turns toward her with a smile. "That should bring the police."

Irina trains her gun on Saxon. "Are you going to kill me now?"

"That depends on your answer." Irina coolly awaits the question. "I remember you burning me with a cigarette. While I was being tortured. Did you?"

"I couldn't resist joining in with the fun." Irina smiles. "But that was before I knew you. When you were merely an assignment. Before I realized how interesting you are. Does that mean I get a bullet in the head?"

Saxon lowers the gun. "That means you don't." Saxon looks around the room. "Shino is lying dead somewhere by now. Philip is nearly dead. Obinna is well on the way. Hanako will most likely join them." He looks back to Irina. "You will start to feel uncomfortable yourself in a couple of days."

Irina's composure dissolves as she looks down in horror at Philip and Obinna.

Saxon continues in an emotionless drone. "The virus is transmitted by physical contact. The Doctor was working on an airborne strain, but he never had a chance to perfect it. Whoever tortured me, I'm sure, were professionals. Aware of the dangers that lurk in the human body. I'm sure they took precautions. But not Shino."

•　　　•　　　•

Saxon and Shino make love in her room at the inn.

•　　　•　　　•

"Or Philip and Obinna."

• • •

Philip and Obinna beat up Saxon in the catacombs at Sedlec.

• • •

"Or my two wives."

• • •

In the country cottage Saxon kisses Valeria.

• • •

In the country cottage Saxon kisses Katri.

• • •

"Hopefully, they will find time to be intimate with their husbands before they grow too ill." His cold-blooded recitation is touched with regret. "Hopefully, the little girl will survive."
Irina begins to tremble. "I'm infected."
"Of course."

• • •

Saxon and Irina make love in the back seat of the car on the way to the inn.

• • •

"You've got some time. The virus takes a while when it's not injected directly into a vein. But when it strikes, it's not pretty."
Police sirens sound in the distance.
Irina aims her gun at the middle of Saxon's forehead. "Who ARE you?"
"I am the living death. Other than that, I don't know. My head is a mess."
Hanako staggers to her feet, approaching Saxon as she sobs. "Am I infected?"

"Did you make love to Obinna?"

Her answer is to collapse to the floor in heaving tears.

"There is no cure, Hanako. Except one." Irina kills her with a head shot. She turns the gun back to Saxon. "So you were executing me when we made love in the car." Saxon nods without smiling. "I should execute you now."

"You'd be doing me a favor. Typhoid Mary didn't live to be an old woman. The disease eventually got her. It took a few months. And I'm sure those months weren't pleasant."

"We're both walking dead, then." Irina's gun wavers, but it doesn't lower. "Strange bonds can develop between captor and captive. I have come to care for you, Saxon. So I will do you that favor." Irina fires.

Saxon reflexively returns fire. He hits her between the eyes, and she falls, while her bullet goes into the wall behind him.

Obinna, balled up in agony on the floor, looks up at the sound of gunfire. "She missed?" he gasps. "She never misses."

"She didn't miss. She hit what she was aiming for."

Police sirens are very loud now. Saxon drops the gun and walks out the door. Leaving the door open, he walks down the hall. It is deserted. He walks into the lobby. The desk clerk is behind the front desk with a gun pointed at Saxon. Saxon pauses to smile at him. "Inform the police there is a biohazard loose in room one." He walks up to the desk directly before the clerk. "Shoot me if you wish. Just don't let any of my blood get on you." The desk clerk lowers his gun and backs away. Saxon turns and strolls out of the inn.

Saxon walks out into the courtyard. People are scattered about the fringes. The police sirens are SCREAMING as several cars pull up before the inn. Saxon walks through the deserted tables of the courtyard cafe as officers charge into the inn. Reaching the street, he finds the car with the two Americans is gone. But the female tour guide stands beside the car he had arrived in. As Saxon approaches, she pulls out a gun.

Saxon holds out his arms, showing he has no weapon, at least not one he is holding in his hands. "You'd better put that away. This place is swarming with police."

She looks all around in a panic, uncertain what to do. Saxon lunges up to knock the gun from her hand. She steps back, terrified, up against the side of her car — there is nowhere to go.

Smiling like a devil, Saxon steps up to take her in his arms and kiss her. She resists for only a moment before melting in his arms. At last, Saxon leans away, smiling, as she looks up at him with a mix of fear and lust. "I'll miss you. Soon, I hope." Saxon turns and walks off.

Most everyone is going the opposite direction with phones out, rushing toward the courtyard where all the commotion is. Saxon is in no hurry, and is careful to avoid making contact with anyone rushing past him. He arrives at the puppet shop. It is closed. He pauses to admire the puppets displayed in the window. A reflection of a giant bug steps up next to his reflection. "Hello, Gregor."

"What do you intend to do?"

"Find a quiet place to die. Away from everyone."

"I know a stone quarry outside of town."

"Sounds perfect. Lead the way." Saxon and the giant bug walk away from the puppet shop down the narrow streets of old town.

About the Author

Mike Sherer has been writing his entire life. His first published work was a record review column in his college paper. His novels include his paranormal/suspense novel, *A Cold Dish* (James Ward Kirk Fiction), horror novella, *Under A Raging Moon* (World Castle Publishing), paranormal mystery novel, *Souls of Nod* (Breaking Rules Publishing), and his middle grade novel, *Shadytown* (INtense Publications). The movie from his screenplay *Hamal_18* is currently available on Amazon Prime.

Mike Sherer lives in West Chester in the Greater Cincinnati area of southwest Ohio. You can learn more about his works and world on his website *mikesherer.org*.

You Might Also Enjoy

CARNIVAL FARM
by Lisa Jacob

When a local veterinarian decides to take over a traveling carnival's petting zoo, she doesn't realize the insanity behind the scenes.

DANGEROUS INSPIRATION
by Greg Stone

Synesthesia alters detective-turned-novelist Ronan Mezini's perceptions. But can it help him find the killer?

FRUIT OF THE DEVIL
by Mary Flodin

Ms. Aurora Bourne would do anything to protect her students from harm … even if that means going up against the most powerful corporation on the planet.